# Intoxinated

# Intoxinated

*an urban fantasy*

## Kenton E. Biffert

**To order additional copies of this book, contact:**
Xlibris Corporation
1-888-795-4274
www.Xlibris.com
Orders@Xlibris.com
48449

Dedicated to Dolan Eagles (1984-2004)

*Your laughter will always be in my heart.*

Special Thanks to Lee Ann Waines for the tireless hours she spent with *Intoxinated*. It lives because of her.

To Joan Scott, Domenic Smith, Sydney Malyon, Skylar Roth-MacDonald, Madison Herbert, Paul Boultbee, Dave Schumacher, Kesha Konowalyk, Kaylee Konowalyk, and the beautiful Rebecca Biffert for their input and investment into this novel.

To the Roman Catholic Church for bringing me home.

To the Eagles family, especially Keenan and Carlee who let their names stand as characters in this novel.

To Laurie Herzog for the great sketches.

To my children Winter and Tristan, that they may some day love literature as much as their daddy.

To my wife for her unfailing support and love of her intense husband.

# Intoxinated

*The Purging: Book 1*

# PART I

*The Source*

# Chapter One

Red Deer, AB
Highland Green
June 15
7:20 am

Dolan stood on the North Hill looking over the City of Red Deer. The sun was a bright red circle. Rising in the East, it cast a pink glow over the city below. The city's tallest buildings, the hospital and a hotel on what was known as the South Hill, caught the glow in their windows and lit them up like beacons of fire. Today was going to be hot, Dolan could feel it.

Red Deer was a brilliant city. It was small enough to be able to drive across in about twenty minutes, yet its population of 85,000 was large enough to support plenty of chain stores and amenities. Dolan stretched and let the morning sunlight chase away his chill. He looked down into the valley, the city's heart, where the Red Deer River, wound its way. Lazy it was. It hardly ever ran fast and it wasn't very deep. The river, easygoing, gentle and calm, truly personified the character of Red Deer. Every summer, it carried hundreds of floaters and rafters through the city to a park called Three Mile Bend. If you didn't have the money to get a dingy, you could swim down the river through the city. Dolan knew this—he'd done it a few times. Dolan looked down at the old trestle bridge stretching over the river. His mom told him there used to be a train that ran over that bridge and through the city. You could hop on it in Lower Fairview and ride it all the way to the south side. That'd be sweet. The city had taken the rails out long ago, and the trestle bridge was now a walking bridge. A great bridge! A place for wedding pictures, a ledge to jump from into some of the river's deeper waters, a railing for lovers to lean against and whisper. Sitting on the grass, dew soaking his pants, Dolan pulled his knees up to his chest and sighed. This was a good place to be. This was his city. He had roamed every alley, every bike trail, every park . . . he felt safe . . . confident . . . .

Today, this would change.

10:06 am

The cigarette hung limply from her dry lips. The cotton aftertaste that comes from a night of drinking mixed with the flavour of the smoke as it curled down into her lungs and out again. Greedily, the smoke reached out its hands and clung to her hair . . . to her worn black tank top . . . to the green paisley couch . . . and to her son. Brushing her curly hair out of her eyes, Lori took the cigarette out of her mouth, reached down and butted it out on their golden carpet. Keenan watched his mom from where he was sitting wedged in between the couch and coffee table.

*She looks so tired,* he thought. Reaching over, he dutifully grabbed the crushed butt from the floor and dropped it into a mug on the table.

Lori leaned forward, moved some of last night's now-empty beer cans from their cluttered, second-hand coffee table and put her feet up. Running her hands through her dishevelled, black hair, she sighed, flipped the TV channels again and lit up another cigarette.

Keenan watched his mom silently, knees pulled up against his chest as he leaned his back against the base of the couch. He waited patiently for the next cigarette butt.

Lori flipped through some channels, slouched a bit lower and let out a long breath of smoke.

Carlee, Keenan's 13-year-old twin, lifted her head slightly to hear what was playing on the television.

*Mom will be sleeping soon,* she thought.

Sitting cross-legged on a worn, stained mattress in the room that she and Keenan shared at night, she flipped absent-mindedly through a teen magazine. A poster of 2PAC, lifting up his shirt to show off his gangster abs, hung on the wall. Below the room's only window, a red thumbtack held a frame made of green and red construction paper. It had a picture of Carlee and Keenan in the middle and in sparkled glue said 'We love you mom!'

*Greedily, the smoke reached out its*
*hands and clung to her hair . . .*

Carlee looked down at her arm and traced a finger around the most recent burn mark. It was red and the small hairs on her dark-skinned arms were singed. Carlee grabbed her long dark hair streaked with blond and lifted it up into a bun on the back of her head. She let herself fall backwards into the mattress and closed her eyes.

Stepping out the front door, Dolan turned to look back at his brother and his mom. He opened his mouth to say good-bye, thought better of it, and shut the screen door quietly. Jumping the three stairs to the pavement, he took off running to the back of the duplex to find his friends. Waiting and leaning up against the tired fence were Brooks and Brandon, his best friends. Dolan smiled as he walked up. He not only was a full foot taller, but a year older than them at fifteen. His buzz cut hair, long arms, dark skin, and baggy clothes left the impression of a hoodlum to the casual observer. Until they saw his smile. Dolan's smile stretched across his face, lit up his eyes, and drew people easily into his confidence—a character trait he often used to his advantage.

*This is going to be fun,* he thought to himself. "Hey guys!" he yelled out loud.

Brooks and Brandon both turned around and looked at Dolan expectantly. Dolan lifted up a crowbar from the ground, and waved it in the air. "Today we're going to have an adventure!"

Dolan's yell carried through the broken basement window into Tyler's bedroom. A groan escaped his lips as he raised his pulsating head from the pillow to look at the time. The clock read 10:10 am. Gingerly he laid his head back down and smacked his lips trying to encourage saliva into his fuzzy mouth. Running his teeth along his tongue, he scraped off a slight film and spit it against the basement wall. His saliva was still slightly bloody. Tyler looked up into the unfinished basement ceiling and ran his fingers over the sparse stubble on his chin. Voices from the TV filtered through the heating vents . . . *What is mom watching?* Tyler wondered. Exhausted, he closed his eyes. In his mind, he saw images of the night before . . . .

*Lots of cigarette smoke from lots of people filled the house. Cases of beer cans were stacked in available spaces such as on the television, on the flat garbage can lid, and strewn amidst the condiments in the refrigerator. Mom's friends, ex-boy friends, and friends she didn't know yet filled the room and poured out into the front yard. Parties meant free beer for Tyler and his friends. The grownups always laughed when they saw him drinking beer. 'Just like Lori,' they always said.*

*It felt good to be accepted by the grownups. It felt good to be like his mom.*

*As the night wore on, the guests became more intoxicated. Their voices became louder; fights broke out here and there. A light bulb smashed in the living room. Brad, mom's ex, motioned to the bathroom.*

*"Don't drink all the beer!" he shouted obnoxiously. They laughed. He had stumbled drunkenly over to the hallway.*

*Something hadn't felt right to Tyler. He had waited. When Brad didn't return, Tyler gritted his teeth and decided to check things out. He walked down the darkened hallway. He could see the bathroom door. It was open and the room was unoccupied. He stopped. Holding his breath, he listened hard. Sure enough, after a moment he heard Brad's muffled voice through his sister's bedroom door. Brad was speaking in a low, but threatening tone. ". . . cry? I'll do it again and again . . . come on . . . brat!"*

*Tyler pushed the door open just in time to see Brad pressing a cigarette into the tender flesh of his sister's forearm. Tyler's vision had blurred as he struggled to contain his fury. Fists swinging, he flew at his sister's tormentor. He cursed and swore as he struck the larger man's torso and biceps again and again. With an amused snort, Brad had thrown Tyler down as easily as Tyler himself might have flicked away a fly. Pinned to the ground, Tyler was helpless. Brad's heavy fists connected solidly with his face.*

*Confident that he had won, Brad got up. He stumbled to the corner of the room, unzipped his pants and urinated down the wall and onto the floor. Mumbling curses as he zipped himself up, Brad left the room.*

*Tyler lay still for a moment longer before looking around for Carlee. She was huddled in the closet.*

*"Find Keenan and stay downstairs for the night, you understand?" Carlee nodded, slipped past Tyler, and went cautiously outside into the hallway.*

That had been last night. Tyler carefully shifted his swollen head on his pillow and went back to sleep.

# Chapter Two

June 15
10:30 am

Brandon, red hair dancing in every direction, freckles covering his cheeks and nose, stood next to his shorter, and rounder friend Brooks. Both of them rested their hands on top of the fence that surrounded the Featherclaw's yard. Together they watched Dolan, the second oldest Featherclaw, approach.

"What's the pipe for?" Brandon called.

"It's a crowbar you idiot," laughed Brooks. Brandon turned and shoved him away from the fence. Dolan marched up with eyes gleaming in anticipation.

Running his hands over his shaved head and wiping the sweat on his pants, he gestured down the alley to a manhole—"Boys we gonna' find Ninja Turtles!"

*    *    *

Carlee rubbed her hands down her arms. She looked down at the burn mark on her left arm. Gently she touched it. She cringed slightly from the pain.

Acknowledging the hunger pangs in her stomach, she rolled off her mattress. She went across the discoloured, laminate floor and into the kitchen. The place was a mess. Empty beer cans, liquor bottles, and chip bags littered the floor. Standing on her tiptoes, she reached up to a cupboard above the sink and grabbed an open bag of cookies. Seeing her mom on the couch and Keenan on the floor, she sat quietly next to her mother, resting her right arm on her mom's lap.

"Good morning Mom."

"Good morning Carlee." The words were forced, but gentle.

Carlee reached into the bag and placed a cookie in her mom's hands. As her mom ate the cookie, Carlee changed positions so that she was sitting on her knees. She began to untangle her mom's thick hair.

"Did you have fun at the party, Mom?"

"Hmmm . . . . mmm," her mom answered with a shrug, "I like it when you play with my hair honey."

Carlee smiled. "I like it to."


Keenan sat and watched their interactions. He looked up at Carlee. Carlee smiled. Keenan and Carlee understood each other. Being twins, they experienced everything in life together. They were in the same class at school, they shared the same bedroom, and they were similar in personality—both gentle and easygoing. Their eyes were like their mother's—a rich dark chocolate with long eyelashes. Every summer, their native skin went from lightly toasted to well done. The fraternal twins were close to the same height, and both had smiles that could light up a room. Their hair was thick and black like their mothers. Carlee's was long and straight, Keenan's curled the longer it got.

Keenan broke eye contact. Looking down, he searched absently for more cigarette butts on the carpet.

*    *    *

The underground was thick with a musty, dank smell. The stink became sourer as Dolan descended into the manhole.

They lived in Highland Green, an older area of Red Deer. The manholes, therefore, still had the older-style big grates. They came off easily, unlike the newly-styled ones with the five holes.

Brooks, with his spiked, dyed blond hair came down next. Being a bit chunkier and shorter than the other two, the going was a bit slower. As Brooks climbed down, Brandon followed. Brandon sunk into manhole and stopped at eye level. With his flaming red, dishevelled hair, he looked somewhat like a curious rooster poking its head out of the ground. Bracing his back against the one side of the hole and his feet against the other, he used both of his arms to drag the manhole cover back into place. He let it drop with a clang and manoeuvred it slightly so there was enough room to get his hand back through for when they came back.

Brooks spoke quietly as Brandon descended, "Man, it stinks down here."

"Yeah, quit your farting Brandon," Dolan grunted loudly.

"Take off!" was the only retort that Brooks and Dolan heard. The three of them laughed.

Twelve rungs later, Dolan called a halt.

"'Kay guys, I can see the bottom, but I gotta drop off the last rung to get there."

"I don't know about this . . ." Brandon whispered, uneasiness edging into his voice, "Let's just head back up. What if we can't get back up 'cause the rung is too high? What if a car parks over manhole cover? What do we do when the light runs out? What if we—"

"Shut up!" barked Brooks. He also was feeling a bit nervous but he didn't want to show it. His hands became sweaty and he wiped them on his jeans.

Dolan looked up squinting his eyes as the sun shone down the manhole shaft, "Give me your belt Brandon."

"Huh?"

"Give me your belt." I need it to tie on to the end of this last rung as a marker and a way to get back up," Dolan explained.

"But . . . but why don't you use your own belt?"

"My pants will fall off," Dolan retorted, "Now give me your belt."

Brandon unstrung his belt, tested his pants to make sure that they would stay up, and handed it down all the while grasping tightly to the rung. Brooks, beneath Brandon, grabbed the belt and passed it down to Dolan. Dolan, straddling the last rung, tied the belt to the rung and pulled on it tentatively.

"I think it'll hold," he said excitedly.

"Then go," Brooks urged him.

Dolan took one last look up the shaft, nodded to the silhouettes of Brooks and Brandon, and lowered himself down.

*     *     *

Two p.m. rolled around. Tyler stared at his digital night clock. His head felt less foggy, but was still tender where Brad had punched him. *I hate that loser*, thought Tyler. Stretching as he got out of bed, he looked for something to wear. Finding a yellow skate shirt on the floor, he whiffed the armpits, shrugged, and donned it. Tyler went upstairs to find Keenan.

Keenan was sitting up against the couch with his arms resting on his knees. Carlee was cuddled up against Lori who, was breathing softly, head lolled back against the couch cushions, fast asleep. The TV was on, but no one was watching. He plopped down on the couch. Tyler wore his long hair tied back in a ponytail as a silent tribute to his native heritage. He spread his arms out across the back of the couch as he surveyed the room. His gaze rested on a broken bulb in the corner, and then moved to a leaning stack of empty beer cans.

"Any smokes left?" Tyler asked. Keenan didn't look up, but just shook his head.

"Hmph." Tyler stretched and knelt forward on his knees. "Have you rolled any smokes lately, Keenan?" He smacked his lips and looked around for a glass to put some water in.

Keenan slipped a hand into his pocket and pulled out a cigarette. The one end was twisted tightly.

"That's my bro." Tyler lit up, and blew smoke upwards towards the ceiling. "I'm going to need more than this. You know that right?"

Keenan brought his legs up closer to his chest.

Tyler thumped him with his foot in the back of his head. "I'm going to need more smokes. You know that, right?" His tone was serious. "We're going to visit Old Man Chin again when I'm done here. Understand?"

Keenan gave a curt nod, his head still turned to watch the television.

Chey Chin, or Old Man Chin as the local boys called him, owned the North Hill Store. It was a convenience store with an old Coca Cola sign above the door. The windows were protected by painted white mesh, and there were large circular mirrors posted high on the ends of aisles one and four. The North Hill Store was often frequented by boys with no money. It supported the nicotine addiction for many of them.

"You or me this time?" Keenan asked as they approached the store from the rear alley. Keenan's eyes were watchful. This was not something that Keenan enjoyed, however, he understood why they had to do it. They had no money. It was a part of their life.

"I will," said Tyler simply. They stopped behind the store to wait.

*     *     *

Carlee flicked through the channels while her mom slept. Taking a break, she watched her mom. Her mouth hung open revealing teeth stained from years of tobacco use. Her dark curly hair hung loosely over dark native skin. Black bags hung like pirate patches beneath her eyes and her clothes hung off her gaunt frame. Carlee took in a deep breath trying to ignore the pains in her stomach. She looked for a third time at the clock and hoped Keenan would be back soon. Carlee hated it when Tyler forced Keenan to steal. Climbing off the couch, she picked up Keenan's mug of cigarette butts. Pulling out the top one, she unwrapped it, letting the unsmoked tobacco grains fall to the table. She picked out another one. This second butt hadn't been smoked nearly as much. Breaking off the filter, she dumped the grains onto this previous pile. *Soon enough,* Carlee thought absently.

# Chapter Three

June 15
2:00 pm

The blackness was thicker than Dolan expected. Sludge grabbed at his feet like goblin arms reaching to pull him under. Phosphorescent slime hung here and there on the walls of the tunnels. It provided a faint glow, which was enough for Dolan to see by as he crept forward. He heard a splunk behind him as Brooks dropped and then another as Brandon followed.

"Gaaaahhh . . . this sucks," grumbled Brandon as put his hand on the cold cement wall of the tunnel to help keep his balance. He quickly removed his hand, now black with slime.

"Give me your shirt Brooks."

"Use your own, eh?"

"Bah," Brandon grumbled and wiped his hand down the side of his pants.

"Come on guys," Dolan encouraged, "this is going to be an adventure."

Shivering slightly, the three boys crept forward down the tunnel.

They never in their wildest dreams imagined just how adventurous things would get.

As their eyes adjusted, they explored their surroundings. The cement walls were curved creating a circular tunnel. Black stains streaked the concrete in various patterns from years of street sewage passing through them. The floor was thick with sludge. It was chilly, but not so cold that they could see their breath. The three of them looked forward in the dark and saw the tunnel curve up ahead.

"Well, Ninja Turtles?" Dolan looked at his friends, "Maybe we'll find Shedder to battle or something, eh?" Brooks stepped closer to the wall to look at the phosphorescent slime clinging there. It glowed slightly.

"What do you think this stuff is?" he called to Dolan up ahead. Dolan and Brandon also stopped to look at the goop on the walls.

"No idea. Toxic waste probably—don't touch it whatever you do."

"Yeah," Brandon replied rewiping his hands on his pants, "I've heard that toxic waste can make you deformed. It's radiation can even mutate brain cells."

Brooks looked at Brandon, "Where in the world did you hear that?"

Brandon shrugged, "Mom has magazines about all kinds of crazy things."

Brooks shook his head, "Weird."

Brandon looked one last time at the glowing goop and followed Dolan.

The minutes ticked by. Some in laughter, and some in curious exploring. Others passed in quiet reflection.

Brandon broke the present silence. "What happens if we get caught down here?"

Dolan shrugged, "Not much. You promise not to do it again and they slap you on the hand." The three of them laughed. By now, they were huddled together with their arms supporting each other so they wouldn't slip and fall into the mire. They turned corners into darkness and searched for the next manhole by the glow of the slime on the walls.

Eventually, their excitement quieted and they fell into a rhythm. The three boys trudged forward toe to heel through the sludge. The air was humid and their lungs laboured from the exertion. Light from the shafts, like the one they had climbed down lit the tunnel sporadically. Otherwise, they depended on the luminous slime slathered in small blobs against the walls.

"Stop," panted Brandon, "I'm tired." The three boys halted. They were at an intersection where three tunnels converged into one main area. The area seemed to be a sort of holding area for sewage water. There were deeper puddles that they had to side step around. The sludge was thicker and it made walking more difficult. The boys were cold. Their shirts were damp with sweat, and Brandon's hair was sticking to his face. Brooks began to shiver.

"Let's get out of here," Brooks suggested.

Dolan looked at the two of them. "Yeah, we've gone far enough—all the tunnels are the same."

"What more did you expect?" Brooks asked.

"I was kinda hoping for an area we could call our own. A hide out, maybe a fort kind of place, you know? But," he lifted up a foot sopping with sludge, "I ain't stayin' down here with all this crap. Who knows how much poop we are actually walking in."

"I wonder where these three tunnels come from," Brooks gestured to the three branches, "maybe from different parts of the city?" Dolan and Brandon looked at the three of them. They moved into a position to look down all three tunnels. Each was dark, and round and identical.

"The big question is, where does this main tunnel lead? Probably to the river, I bet. I actually wouldn't mind following it." Dolan said.

Brandon grimaced. "Uh, no. Let's just go back. I'm cold, hungry and filthy," saying this Brandon turned sharply down the first tunnel and began to walk back.

Dolan called out, "Hey, Brandon. We just came out of this tunnel." He was pointing to the tunnel in the middle, "This is the tunnel we just walked out of."

"Uh, no we didn't." Brandon called back over his shoulder, shook his head and kept walking.

Brooks looked down both tunnels, "Do either of the tunnels have footprints?" All three boys stopped and looked into the sludge for traces that they may have left behind. The muck was so sloppy that their footprints had filled in almost as quickly as they had been left.

Dolan stood up, "Ok, I'm pretty sure we came down this second one—this is my first instinct. Why do you think that we came down the first tunnel?"

Brandon turned, walked back to the boys and answered, "Because we came into this main area and . . ." he closed his eyes trying to remember, "And there were . . . the other tunnels?"

Dolan rolled his eyes. "Brooks?"

Brooks shook his head. "I don't know at all. I had my head down and was following you two. I didn't pay any attention."

The three boys looked at each other and the first vestiges of fear began to curdle their stomachs.

Dolan spoke up, "Brandon, think. Why do you remember that tunnel as the tunnel you were in?"

"Because I remember . . . walking on the left hand side and there was dirt and glowing . . . ," his voice faded out as he realized that, the left hand wall of the tunnels were probably all the same.

"So what do we do now?" Brooks was standing in the intersection with his hands on his hips.

Dolan answered, "Why don't we split up for 10 minutes and then retrace back to this spot. I'll continue down this tunnel, Brandon you continue down yours—but only for 10 min. Brooks, you can go down the third tunnel. After 10 minutes we all turn around and come right back to this spot with what we found. Look for a manhole you recognize or some detail that you noticed." Brandon and Brooks looked doubtful. "Any better suggestions?"

They both shook their heads.

"All right then. Let's find our way out of this joint." The boys trudged off. Each in a different direction, each alone with their thoughts, each hoping they would find something familiar that would lead them out of the maze.

*"So what do we do now?"*

Brooks walked for a ways down the third tunnel, but saw nothing of significance. He *knew* that this tunnel was not the one they came down. After about six minutes, he turned around and headed back to the intersection. Standing now where they all had just been, he lifted his foot. He watched the mud slag off his shoes and slap back into its home. He waited. He waited and fidgeted. He leaned on his knees and wished he could just sit down. After this, he found a spot to lean against the tunnel with his back against the cement. The cold immediately seeped through his cotton shirt. He began to shiver. *This is taking too* long, he thought. Stepping forward, he went down the middle tunnel to meet up with Dolan.

Brandon stopped for a breather and meticulously tried to rid himself of the mud and slime on his clothes. With his forefinger and thumb pinched together, he scraped stubborn clumps of mud off his shirt. He had been walking for about seven minutes and had seen nothing of significance until now. He was at a spot where the tunnel split into two. Brandon stuck to the right, thinking it seemed more obvious that they came from that direction. He continued walking.

"I don't want to get lost," Brandon voiced softly to himself. His arms were shivering and he rubbed them to get the goose bumps to go away. "I don't know if this is the right tunnel," he said aloud again to himself, "It all looks the same." He backed up to the tunnel wall and took a moment to lean against the chilly cement. He closed his eyes and let the cold penetrate his shirt and burn his skin. He tightened his shoulders but relaxed when the initial cold subsided. His thoughts wandered aimlessly. Hunger pangs reminded him that he hadn't eaten in a while, and the mud caked to his body was testament to his need for a hot bath. For a moment he stood, eyes closed, and breathed.

"I just want to get out of here," he said aloud. Having made this conclusion, he turned to his left towards the intersection and stopped.

Brandon looked right. Left. "Stink." Sweat began to wet his palms. His stomach knotted. He realized that he didn't know which way he had just come from. He was second guessing his instinct to go left. Brandon looked for a sign, anything . . . the tunnels seemed to be darker than they were before. He looked down and the footprints where he was just standing had already filled in with watery sludge. Brandon grew weak. He called out weakly, "Dolan? Brooks? Guys?" His voice echoed and fell flat in the still air.

Silence. "HEY GUYS!" Brandon's voice bounced all around him like a bunch of mocking children. "I'm down this tunnel. Help. Dolan? Brooks?"

Brandon stared into the blackness ahead. He couldn't see much more than a few feet ahead. He moved forward and looked down again. Nothing. "Rrrrr!" He kicked the sludge in frustration spraying mud against the walls.

"Guys?" Brandon's voice was a little less sure this time. Fear, with its icy fingers, crept slowly. It gripped his stomach first, and soon held his heart in its claws. Brandon felt on edge. Warm tears threatened to leak out of the corner of his eyes. He stood, frozen. He lost all sense of direction and just stood.

"Be strong. Be strong. I'll be fine. Don't cry." Brandon began to mumble under his breath.

"Be strong. Be strong. I'll be fine. Don't cry." He said it again. The mantra forming . . .

"Be strong. Be strong. I'll be fine. Don't cry."

Brandon forced his tears back, and stood there, arms wrapped around himself and repeated his mantra over and over.

# Chapter Four

June 15<sup>th</sup>
2:00 pm

Skulking under the weather-worn awning in the back alley, Tyler and Keenan watched the people go by. The local Dawe community school had gotten out early today, so there were plenty of teens hanging out. The idea was to enter when there was a fairly large group of people in the building. Old man Chin was too cheap to hire help, which meant that he was always alone, and vulnerable. The difficult part was to get Chin out from behind the counter where the cigarettes were laid out in rows.

Eight minutes went by as the boys counted the customers . . . "3 out . . . 2 in . . . 3 in . . . 2 out . . . we are at 3 . . . 2 in . . . , 3 out . . . , 5 going in . . .—let's go!" Dashing around to the front of the store, they braked at the door and nonchalantly walked in with the five. Swiftly, Keenan headed left down the cereal aisle.

The inside of the store had five aisles, and the cereal aisle was the second furthest from the counter. Stopping in the aisle, Keenan pressed himself against the steel shelves. He picked up the box and pretended to study the price. Reaching deeper into the shelf, he carefully shuffled the cans of tomatoes facing the other aisle, over to the side. He now had a clear line of sight to the checkout and more importantly to the cigarette shelf behind it.

Tyler sauntered amongst the group of five that had flowed into the corner store. Walking slightly behind them, he picked out the biggest kid. Eyes wary, he watched as 'Mr. Big kid' rounded the first aisle and then the second. Tyler left the group and walked around to meet Mr. Big as he stepped around the corner. He smacked hard into the kid's chest and then threw himself back into a stack of canned dog food. SMASH! Dozens of cans crashed to the ground and around Tyler.

"Watch out you loser! Feet too big for you?" Tyler hollered mockingly at the stunned Mr. Big. Jumping up, Tyler threw himself at the kid. Mr. Big, still a bit flabbergasted threw up his hands in defence. A stream of curses flew from Tyler's mouth as he was pushed away. Old man Chin came around the corner in a whir.

"You. Stop fighting you. Pick up cans. Stop. No more of this."

Keenan, seeing the abandoned counter, dashed around to grab a handful of cigarette packages and then swiftly headed back outside. Once he was sure that he was safe, Keenan slowed to a saunter. He hid the goods under his clothing, and walked down the alley towards their house.

Four minutes later, Tyler showed up, huffing.

"Well?" he asked with a smirk on his face. Keenan produced the packs.

"Brilliant work my brother," he exclaimed as he slapped one pack back into Keenan's hand, "Brilliant work."

Laughing to himself, Tyler sat on the step of their house. He lit up and felt the nicotine soothe his craving. Keenan stepped past Tyler, hid his pack under his clothing, and went into the house to find Carlee. He had a different craving that needed to be worked out.

*The North Hill Store was often frequented
by boys with no money.*

\*      \*      \*

Carlee watched Keenan come in from outside. He sat down on the worn golden carpet and began to sift through a small pile of cigarette butts. He broke off the filters and poured whatever tobacco remained out into a small pile. Crawling off the couch, Carlee grabbed a few butts to help Keenan finish. She glanced out the door to Tyler smoking and looked at Keenan. Keenan nodded and patted his shirt where the pack was hidden. Carlee pulled out rolling papers from her mom's purse and she and Keenan proceeded to roll the tobacco into new cigarettes. Silently, they fell into a rhythm—both very comfortable with each other. Hands moving, and eyes focused they put together a total of eight full cigarettes. Those, plus the new pack, gave them a total of thirty-three. Silently, they left their mom sleeping, slipped on their lace-less shoes and headed out.

"Buy a cigarette, sir?" Carlee asked an older guy with stringy grey hair.

"Hurmph," he responded, without even looking at Carlee.

"Cigarette, ma'am?" Keenan held out his hand to a lady with an overly large flowered hand bag.

Hand bag lady paused, looked Keenan up and down and with a stern eye, "One dollar and no more."

"Done." Keenan took the loonie and popped it into his pocket. Hand bag lady hurried off.

"Cigarette, sir?"

"Cigarette, ma'am?"

"Hey, cigarette?"

"Do you want a smoke?"

Within the hour twelve dollars in change jiggled in their pockets. Counting the loonies twice and tucking them into Keenan's zipper pants pocket (so they didn't accidentally fall out) they both headed off past the North Hill store, down the hill to the gas station at the bottom. Walking in politely, they looked eagerly at the food they could purchase. Checking up and down the aisles, they counted out four apples, a box of granola bars, a loaf of raisin bread, and a small bag of gummy bears. After paying and collecting their thirty-two cents in change, they headed back to their house munching on the apples to soothe the hunger pangs in their stomachs.

*   *   *

Waiting and shivering, Dolan and Brooks shuffled their feet in the sludge. Brooks had met up with Dolan coming back to the intersection in the tunnels.

"I'm thinking that's about long enough, eh?" Brooks stopped and placed his hand on Dolan's shoulder. He could feel Dolan shivering in his t-shirt.

"Yeah," agreed Dolan, "There's nothing much we can do here. Brandon must've been right, but where is that bum?"

"Should we wait or go after him?" Brooks was shivering as well.

"We'd better wait. If there are branches in the tunnels, we won't know which ones he took and we could miss each other. The plan was to meet here in ten minutes. We should stick with the plan." Their feet were freezing and sopping from the muck that had penetrated into their shoes.

"Brandon!" Dolan's voice was clear and loud. "Brandon!" Dolan looked at Brooks, and called again, "Brandon—stop playing around! This isn't a joke! Get out here!"

All they heard back was Dolan's own echo. Then silence.

Dolan and Brooks began to shiver harder.

"We've g-got to k-keep moving, we g-got to s-stay warm," Brooks was hugging himself and rubbing the goose bumps on his arms.

"You're right. L-let's walk back and forth down the t-tunnel Brandon went down, but we stick to the plan," Dolan broke into a fit of coughing and shivered as the cold spread down his back, "Come on."

Silently, they began to walk through the sludge down the same tunnel that Brandon went down.

"Do you think he's hurt?" Brook's question hung in the air silently. The question was out there now. Neither of them answered. Their imaginations concocted scenes which played like movies through their brains: *Brandon lying face down in the sludge . . . unconscious . . . Mrs. Bradley crying over a coffin . . .*

Instinctively, they shuffled a bit closer together. They scanned the walls and the ground for any sign of Brandon as they walked. Occasionally they would call out his name, but the sound of their voices seemed to die right in front of them. They walked until the first branch in the tunnel and then walked back to the main intersection. There was still no sign of Brandon. Confused and worried, Dolan and Brooks kept moving to stay warm and kept waiting for Brandon to appear.

# Chapter Five

June 15<sup>th</sup>
2:48 pm

The day shift. Fred Janesen hated it. When he had taken his job as the 'Water Flow Safety Officer' he had been quite content to work nights. Until now. Staffing shortages had made it necessary for the crews to extend, switch and cover shifts 'as needed'. For Fred, 'as needed' was getting to be a major cramp in his style. He was a night owl, and couldn't get his body turned around. The night before, he had been up late. Really late. As a result, he had struggled all afternoon to keep his head from bobbing forward, until finally he couldn't keep his eyes open any longer. Nodding off to sleep, Fred slumped forward in his chair. His head rolled to the side and then rested down. His chair became stressed as the dead weight of Fred's large belly sunk into it. His left hand resting on the sewage control switch, slipped down as his body slumped into blessed sleep. The control switch slipped into the open position. The gates beneath the water treatment plant edged open and 360 tonnes of street sewage began to pour into the underground system.

# Chapter Six

June 15<sup>th</sup>
2:50 pm

The cold was nearly unbearable. Together, Brooks and Dolan peered into the darkness around them. The glow from the goop cast minimal light into their situation.

"Well, what direction do you think we should go in?" Brooks' face betrayed the worry he was feeling.

"Brandon!" Dolan's voice echoed and died ominously in the distant tunnels.

Silence. "Where the stink did he go?" Dolan's anger was becoming evident, "Why didn't he stay with us? It's not like we were running or anything? How hard is it to simply follow?"

Brooks looked at Dolan. "You told us to separate. We listened to you." Brooks' voice was low. "Now you need to find him." His words were chilling. No words spoken aloud could express the thoughts of fear and worry bouncing around in their minds.

Dolan shook his head, and looked once more down the tunnel. "We'll find him. We won't leave without him. We can't." Dolan did one last look around the tunnels all converging in the intersection. "We won't split up this time, and we'll find him."

Brooks and Dolan turned into the tunnel that Brandon went down. "We'll explore this main one until it splits and we'll keep to the left," he said. Brooks nodded and followed.

The phosphorescent walls glittered as they passed.

Moving silently forward, they hoped to God that they were headed in the right direction. Their passage was slow. The silence was thick in the sewers. They could hear their breathing and sometimes see glimpses of it whenever they walked through colder spots. At times, the silence was so oppressive that it felt like their heads were being squished by a vice-grip and it became difficult to breathe. It was a workout. Despite the cold, both boys were constantly wiping the sweat out of their eyes. Dolan continued to rub his hand over his shaved head and wiped the sweat onto his pants. The breaking of clinging goop to their feet with sucks and pops grew into white static in the back of their subconscious.

Hunger pains gnawed at their stomachs and began to steal away rationality. The sewer channels all looked the same. They passed many ladders up high and always kept looking for a belt dangling off one or any sign of Brandon. No Brandon. No belt. No Brandon. No belt.

Stopping, Brooks stated quietly, "I'm tired." He rested his hands on his knees and searched for some reserves of strength. "Are we going to get out of here?" His voice was softer and Dolan looked up at him in surprise.

He stood up straight and lifted Brooks to a standing position. "We will be fine. It'll all be fine. This is just an adventure, that's all." Slowly a tear traced its way down Brooks' cheek through the grime and dirt. Brooks let the tear tickle his cheek and drop.

"This sucks."

"Yup."

"What should we do?"

"I'm thinking," Dolan replied, "I'm thinking . . . we rest and we go back to the where the tunnel split and take the right side. He has to be down one of these two somewhere."

Brooks rested against Dolan's back and closed his eyes.

"What's that sound?"

"What sound?" Dolan answered.

"Listen."

A distant roar like a muffled storm could be heard coming from somewhere in the tunnels.

"Do you hear it now?"

"Yeah."

"Me too," Brooks hugged himself closely, "I'm not sure . . . that I . . . want to find out what where the sound is coming from."

Neither of them had much choice.

*      *      *

Still standing frozen in one spot, Brandon waited. He remembered one of his summer camp counselor's words of wisdom: "If you are lost—hug a tree." Which of course just meant to always 'stay put' if you were ever lost. Walking around could mean more opportunity to get lost. Brandon smiled as he remembered the younger kids who really believed they should hug the tree. "What if the tree is too big to hug?" one little boy asked innocently. Everyone had laughed. Brandon had laughed too. He wished he hadn't. Who would be laughing at him now he wondered?

Brandon looked around at his surroundings. His eye caught the sparkling glow on the wall. It lingered there. Still holding himself to stay warm, he rubbed his arms and crept closer to the wall of the tunnel. The glowing stuff flitted and sparkled and cast a soft silver glow. Tentatively, he pushed his finger into the glowing slime on the walls.

"What is this?" he wondered aloud.

Coolness spread up his fingers as they touched the slime sprinkled with silver flecks. The flecks began to move, first in circles and then they'd join together. The slime now glowed even brighter as the Silver flecks meshed and collided and vibrated together. Intrigued and spell-bound, Brandon's eyes reflected the glow. His face became lit with a silver flush. The silver stuff splashed light around and in the heart of it was an intense silver glow that was harsh to look at. He drew his finger out and the glow diminished as the silver flecks separated and swam in their murky slime. He rubbed his two fingers together expecting there to be a wetness to wipe off. His finger tip was dry. Again, Brandon put his finger tip into the slime. Again, the glow intensified as the silver ions collided and joined into one conglomeration. He removed his finger. Any fears of being lost in a sewer system were placed on the back burner as Brandon focused his attention on this one blob of glowing slime.

Brandon returned his finger to the slime. This time though, he kept it there longer to watch what would happen. As expected the silver light intensified to a silver core. Brandon waited. The slime also seemed to wait. But then slowly, apprehensively, the slime began to crawl up his finger. Surprised, Brandon jerked away and took a step back from the wall. He began to shake a bit. He turned away from the tunnel wall and stared into the blackness. He could see other spots, also glowing silver, down the tunnels. Some smaller, some larger—but all with that same eerie glow. Brandon looked at his finger and did a mental body check. Everything seemed okay . . . he was pretty sure of that . . . the slime hadn't hurt him . . . it just . . . surprised him. Brandon turned again to the soft glowing phosphorescent slime. Abruptly he put his finger back into the slime and willed himself to stay put. Again the colliding of silver, the bright silver light, a pause and a slow creeping up his finger.

It took an elephant amount of will power to not pull away. He watched in fear and fascination as the slime crawled up his finger and into the palm of his hand. Brandon could feel the coolness spreading to the edges of his fingers and then to his wrist as the glowing, swirling slime settled into his palm. The gelatinous substance lay cradled, as calm as a resting baby. Brandon held up his other hand and let the silver substance slide plop! into it. It moved back and forth between his hands like wet jello, but left no wetness or stickiness. Just a cool feeling remained that spread to the ends of his fingers.

Brandon was completely focused on his discovery. He did not notice the distant din building and reverberating somewhere in the tunnel systems.

# Chapter Seven

June 15<sup>th</sup>
3:18 pm

Hugging each other, Brooks and Dolan shivered and watched the icy, black water climb higher up their calves. At first they were a bit surprised as it had begun to rise a bit over their shoes, but they initially dismissed their worry, thinking it was just wetter in this area of the tunnels. The water continued to rise rather quickly. They were well aware now of the echoes of crashing water as it stormed and bashed its way through the tunnel system.

"We n-need to get out of here Brooks," said Dolan through chattering teeth.

"L-l-l-lets go th-th-then," Brooks stammered, "But what about Brandon?"

"Brandon is on his own now. We have to find that belt or we'll drown. W-w-we don't have a choice." Dolan began to cough and shiver some more.

Water swirled around their legs they slogged and splashed until they came to the next shaft of light from a manhole.

"This will have to do," Dolan speculated. The lowest ladder rung was still four feet above their heads, Looking at the water which was now around their thighs left them both with a sense of foreboding. This wasn't supposed to happen.

"Get on my shoulders," muttered Dolan.

Brooks hesitated.

"NOW!" Dolan's voice echoed loudly and was lost in the din of the storming water.

Brooks scrambled, dripping wet onto Dolan's shoulders, balancing himself with one hand on the wall. Careful to avoid the toxic glowing slime, he inched his way closer and closer to the bottom rung. Knees now on Dolan's shoulders, Brooks wrapped his clammy, muddy hands round the bottom rung.

"I'm here," Brooks exclaimed in short breaths, "I'm here."

"Pull yourself up—quick!" Dolan stole a glace down and grimaced as the cold water gripped his crotch. Brooks wrapped his arms around the rung and with a slippery push off the wall he heaved himself upwards. Cradling the steel bar, he dangled his arms down to Dolan. Two to three feet of air stretched between them.

"Jump!" Brooks called above the rising sound of rushing water. Dolan's body fought to get control. Muscles twitched, contracted, and became weaker with every passing second in the cold water. Fighting the overwhelming urge to collapse, Dolan jumped. His arms waved wildly in the air, missing Brooks by about a foot. He came crashing down into the black water. He rose up sputtering and spewing. Sludge clung to his cheeks and hair. Dolan swayed as the water continued to climb.

Brooks began to panic when he saw that Dolan was fighting to stay conscious.

"DOLAN!" he screamed. The current was getting stronger and Dolan was taking small steps backwards to keep from being washed over. Brooks screamed again.

Dolan looked straight ahead and didn't notice the ever widening distance between himself and his only hope of safety.

"DOLAN! DOLAN! FIGHT!" "SWIM!" Brooks was screaming continually now and tears mixed with water spray that soaked his cheeks as he struggled to get Dolan's attention.

Brooks' voice grew more distant. Dolan closed his eyes. He imagined a large crowd of people jostling and pushing him here and there. *Man it's hard to fight this crowd. I should turn and go with the flow.* He felt so weak . . . so tired . . . . *This crowd is big* . . . He could hear his name being shouted from somewhere in the crowd. *I can't see who it is* . . . Dolan continued to stumble backwards and smacked his shoulder against the tunnel wall. Water was up past his navel, and shivers still wracked his body—though less frequently now. He was feeling numb. Vacant. He opened his eyes and closed them blinking water from them. Turning around, he placed the palms of his hands on the wall, and braced himself. He shook his head to clear his thoughts.

The water continued its rising onslaught, and Dolan found himself searching the walls with his hands for a crack to use as a handhold.

Sharp cold bit into his flesh.

Dolan, suddenly alert, jerked his palms away from the cold cement and recoiled at the glowing slag stuck to his hand. He shook his hand and the slag dropped into the water. Relieved, Dolan continued to run his hands along the tunnel walls, all the while being pulled downstream.

Up ahead, a shaft of sunlight was illuminating a small area of the tunnel. He could see a ladder reaching down which meant that there would be a manhole above.

*This is it. I need to get on this ladder.* Dolan turned downstream and let the water drive him. The shaft came closer and the first vestiges of light touched his skin. It was a welcome relief from the inky blackness of the tunnels. He began to jump, using his buoyancy to give him a bit more height. The ladder loomed. Dolan dug his feet into the floor of the tunnel and with a hard push, he propelled himself into the air. Both hands swept through air just beneath rungs and with a SPLASH he plummeted down back into the rushing waters.

Frantically, he brought his head to the surface and ran his hands over his face. He turned. The manhole was behind him now. He felt desperate. The water continued to push and shove him, lifting him off his feet. Dolan raked his hands along the tunnel walls looking for a crack or a handhold. Instead he ended up grabbing fistfuls of the silver slime. Although his hands were nearly numb with cold, he could still feel the slick cool of the slime. It was almost as though . . . as though he could sense it.

He was now half swimming and half hopping off the bottom of the tunnel trying to keep his balance. He flung the silver stuff off his hands and wiped them on his wet clothes. The glowing substance bobbed and floated away. Dolan watched it. Fighting to stay upright, Dolan grabbed another fistful of slime and threw it into the water. It too bobbed, and then flowed with the current into the darkness.

Then it hit him.

He maneuvered himself to the tunnel walls and began raking his hands along them. He gathered as much slime as he possibly could. Anxiously, he grabbed fistful after fistful and rubbed it all over his clothes and filled up his pockets. A vague sense of uncertainty gnawed at him, but was quickly drowned out by the direness of the situation. Survival instinct and adrenaline surged through him. It was get out or drown. Dolan's core body temperature began to rise as blood and adrenaline flowed through his muscles. They became limber again as he fought the current to stay close to the tunnel walls. Then he felt it. He was beginning to float. His body was becoming more and more buoyant. The stuff was working!

Dolan began to swim and bounce off of the walls. The effort to keep afloat was becoming less and less. He allowed himself to rise to the top.

He couldn't believe it. Floating easily, he relaxed a bit and began to settle slightly into the murky, ever rising water. He was being carried through a maze of tunnels and he no longer resisted the pull of the deluge. His only concern was to try to keep his head above the water line.

*I need more of this slime*, thought Dolan.

Dolan moved closer to the tunnel's side. He scraped more slime from the walls and began to stuff more of it into his pockets.

Dolan didn't know what the consequence of using this slime was going to be, but now he only needed to live. If it had any effect, he'd deal with it later. If there was a later. There had to be a later. Floating in the water, he could see that he was glowing. He was a glowing like an apparition moving through undiscovered depths. The now concentrated mass of Silver cast a glow so bright that seeing in the darkness was not a problem at all. He was a living flashlight.

The water was deep now. Rushing headlong through the channels, Dolan floated. Whenever his face went under, he rose, spewing and spitting. He prayed silently that the water levels didn't rise any higher. Spewing out another mouthful of muddy water, Dolan resigned himself to the current and wondered where he was going to end up.

\*     \*     \*

Brooks cringed as the echo of his screams died off. He saw Dolan scrambling helplessly against the flow. Eventually, arms flailing, Dolan faded into the blackness of the tunnels leaving only the rising water behind him. Dripping and shivering, Brooks clung to his rung with every ounce of his strength. Dirty water dripped from his clothing into the water below. He couldn't help but feel somewhat grateful for the light that shone down through the manhole above.

He began to cry. Brooks felt lost and nearly broken. Sobs wracked his body and his chest heaved in and out against the cold steel rung. Brandon was lost and Dolan was drowning.

He was safe.

Brooks clung to the rung for a long time. The water rose higher and higher. Gaining some measure of control, and yet shivering like a blade of grass on a windy day, he wiped his eyes and blew his nose into the water beneath him. Unwrapping his stiff body, Brooks began his steep ascent to the manhole cover above, wondering how on earth he was going to lift it off and where in the city he'd end up.

\*    \*    \*

Brandon was utterly fascinated. From his hands, the Silver continued to slide upwards. It seemed to inspect his arms and shoulders. It was almost comforting. *This stuff must be reacting to chemicals in my body,* Brandon thought as the followed the Silver's journey. *There is no way it could be alive.* Brandon put his hand like barricade on his shoulder; the silver crawled right up his hand and over it. As the water rose higher and higher, Brandon had to fight to stay in his spot. Momentarily he forgot about the slime as he fought to regain his balance. The slime continued its ascent. At Brandon's neck, it spread out like syrup on a pancake and climbed up his chin.

Brandon fought to stay upright against the water pressing against his legs. Splash! He fell under the water. He couldn't see. His hands touched the bottom of the tunnel. Forcing his fingers into the sludge, he desperately fought for a handhold. Bringing his feet underneath him, he righted himself, eyes squinting in the zero visibility waters, lungs beginning to burn, Brandon propelled himself upward. His head broke the surface and he opened his mouth with a gasp. Welcome air rushed into his lungs, expanding them to capacity before his head submerged again.

Brandon knew he was in trouble. He never had been a strong swimmer—he kept his swimming to the hot tub at the local Recreation Centre pool downtown. Trying to keep his head above water in the ever-rising tide was worse than jumping off the high board at the pool. Again, Brandon righted himself under the water and propelled his body upward. This time however, Brandon broke through the surface and threw his feet forward so he was in a back float position. Sewer water continued to splash over his body and face as he was being swept through the tunnels.

By this time, Silver had crept along Brandon's face, seemingly unaffected by the water. It surrounded his eyes. The red freckles that covered his nose and cheeks were burning under Silver's cover. It circled his nose and mouth so that it looked like he was wearing a silver mask. Then, without warning the Silver gathered itself into one puddle and with a silent whoosh slammed itself down Brandon's throat.

There was a moment of shock before Brandon realized what had happened. Flailing in the water now, Brandon grasped at his throat and rammed his fingers into his mouth to try to catch the intruder. The Silver, cool and fluid, slid down his windpipe and into his lungs. Brandon thumped his chest with his fists, jammed two fingers down his throat and ended up swallowing sewer water. Again his head was submerged.

Brandon's mind went into a frenzy. He had been invaded. His body fought to reject the foreign substance coating his lungs. He could feel a cool burn of the as the substance filled his chest cavity. Screaming for breath, Brandon again found something solid and pushed against it to thrust himself upward.

Smash!

Flashing lights danced before his eyes as lightning bolts of pain shot from his skull and coursed down his neck. Brandon, squeezed his eyes shut and tears began to meld into the torrents of water around him. *I don't know which way is up,* Brandon thought. Panic began to zap his intellect. Desperate now, lungs screaming in pain, Brandon found solid cement under his feet. With a lighter shove, he shot forward, hands above his head. His fingers again touched cement—but no air. Maybe the water has risen to the top . . . *I'm going to die* . . . Brandon's body tensed. Black and green began to form at the edges of his thoughts closing in like elevator doors. Squinting, one more time into the sewage, Brandon thought he saw something floating and glowing in the water. With that last image, his mind deprived of oxygen, Brandon lost.

# Chapter Eight

June 15
3:45 pm

With a jerk, Fred slammed his head up.

"Hiya!" he whispered to himself, "Gotta' have some coffee."

Hefting his large waist off the swivel chair, he grabbed the counter and lifted himself to a standing position. He looked down at his waist, adjusted his belly over his belt, and was about to head out when something stopped him. Something didn't seem right. He looked back at his chair. He felt his back pocket—yup, wallet still there. He ran his roughened hand over the 2-day stubble on this face and looked once more at the control panel. His eyes scanned the controls. They drifted left, then right and landed on the sewage control switch. It was in the open position.

"Hiya!" Fredrick quickly reached over, slammed it into the off position, and looked around to see if anyone noticed. Of course, no one would notice—he was in an office in the back hallway of the water treatment plant—no one would notice. Fred again adjusted his belly, pulled up his faded jeans and nonchalantly swaggered out of his office and down the hallway to the staff room.

Twenty-five feet below, unheard by any staff or water treatment officials, the sewer control grates creaked shut and stunted the water flow.

Twenty-five feet below, two kids, stuck in the sewage system tunnels, were drowning.

# Chapter Nine

June 15
3:50 pm

Brandon's body floated limp in the water, tossed back and forth by the currents and the rushing, rising water. Brandon's mind began to shut down from the lack of oxygen. He resigned his screaming lungs to defeat. Reflexively, his body opened his mouth to breathe in. Suddenly relief poured into his lungs and Brandon's brain jump-started. His mouth snapped shut. Synapses sparked and consciousness streamed back into his being. Silver-toxicated blood began to course through this body feeding life to the suffocating cells.

Brandon tried to stay relaxed. Confusion. What was going on? He was still under water, his mouth was shut, he was dying—drowning—*this is what death must be like. I'm dead, I'm sure of it. This is my soul outside my body watching it float downstream.*

Brandon reached out. His hands touched the side of the tunnel.

*Can souls feel? This feels so real . . . Maybe this is my heaven or . . . purgatory . . .*

Just then a current slammed Brandon's head into the side of the tunnel. A jolt of pain coursed through him and his eyes flew open into the murky water. The water stung and instinctively he reached out to rub them shut.

*I'm alive!*

Brandon wanted to shout. Closing his eyes, he stayed under water and let the current take him down the tunnel. Brandon breathed deeply and paused.

*How am I breathing?*

Still underwater, he reached his hands up to his face—it felt unnaturally cold. His lungs weren't expanding, but his heart was beating. Then Brandon remembered the silver stuff. He remembered the shock of the intrusion, the screaming of his lungs, and the thoughts of dying . . . He was breathing Silver.

*I'm breathing under water!* Brandon was stunned. Bashing and crashing along with the current he mentally did a body check. Hands? Okay. Feet? Okay. Arms? Okay . . . . he seemed all in one piece. Slightly nervous, he let his mind's fingers look into his chest. His lungs. They felt cool, refreshed even after the intense burning. They were breathing. Trying to squint through the murk, another thought, a crazy idea floated to the surface . . . *what if I rub this glowing Silver into my eyes? . . . will I be able to see better, just as I can breathe better? This gloop, this Silver, this stuff is alive or friendly or lonely or something. It doesn't want to hurt me . . . it'll only help me . . .*

Using the current as it swept him around a corner and up against the wall, Brandon grasped and clamped onto some more of the silver saviour. Hesitating slightly, he began to rub the cool ionic substance into his eyes. Immediately the coolness turned to burning and light streaked into his retinas piercing every cone and every nerve. Brandon wanted only to scream.

*   *   *

Slightly in control now, Dolan let his body be carried further and further through the tunnels. Lost? Absolutely. However, being lost was secondary to staying alive. Floating easily at the surface, glowing like a firefly, he watched light from the manholes shining like heavenly beacons into his darkness. The water was still moving too fast to try and climb up to one. Too fast and too deep. Minutes passed. How many minutes? He had no idea. He was cold, frigid and numb. Breathing deeply, Dolan tried to keep control of his shivering limbs.

Dolan blinked some water out of his eyes and looked again down the tunnel. The darkness was getting lighter he noted. There must be another manhole around the next bend.

However, around the next bend was not a manhole, but a grate. The grate was made of rusted rebar and secured to a sewage tunnel opening. Beyond the grate and thirty feet below was the Red Deer River. Water was rushing out of the gate creating a sparkling waterfall in the sunlit afternoon.

Rounding the last bend, sunlight crashed into Dolan's eyes—momentarily blinding him. Squinting he looked forward in hope. The hope bombed and exploded like the water hitting the river below. Caged. Trapped like an animal. Dolan braced his feet ahead of him in a water ski position. The water carried Dolan forward and slammed him into the grate. There was an imperceptible snap as Dolan's ankle cracked and snapped. Pain exploded into his brain and Dolan dropped beneath the water. Screaming inside, Dolan fought to get control. Grabbing the rebar with his hands, he began to pull his body upward. He needed air. His foot now dangling uselessly, Dolan raised his head above the water and breathed. Water flooded over Dolan's head and body rushing out through the grates and dropping into the river below.

Dolan struggled to right himself. Grabbing rusted, rebar grate with his cold fingers, he began to slowly position his body around. His buoyancy worked in his favour and quickly he was standing on one foot, stomach and face pressed hard against the grate. The water rushing over his head created a pocket of air for him to breathe and now Dolan could catch glimpses of the river below. The water flowing past him peeled the Silver from his clothing and sent it sparkling into the river below. The sun's rays created twinkling stars off the spray. Dolan could see and taste his possible freedom behind the bars of his watery prison.

\*      \*      \*

At the top of the steel rung ladder, Brooks pushed his shoulder against the iron cover. No movement. He could see outside the grates. The black tarmac of the road stretched out before him. Leaves and a slurpee cup were jammed and squished up against the curb partially blocking his view.

"Help!" Brooks shouted desperately through the manhole cover. "Help!"

Across the street, an overweight, middle-aged woman with a flowered handbag turned her head.

\*      \*      \*

Glowing silver ions crept their way along the membranes of his eyes, danced on his pupils and formed into a mesh covering. Still breathing under water, Brandon hesitantly opened his eyes in the murk. Light beamed from them and illuminated the area directly in front. There was no stinging, he didn't need to squint—it was as if he was wearing goggles. Shivering, but excited, Brandon continued to swim under the water. He swept his eyes back and forth watching the beams of silver light sweep the tunnel floor. His body was in a state of euphoria. The panic was gone. He looked like a human submarine scouring the bottom of the ocean floor. He began to enjoy his water slide, roller-coaster ride through the undergrounds. Eyes scouring, body twisting, Brandon continued his course through the tunnels. He was going to live.

# Chapter Ten

June 15<sup>th</sup>
4:55 pm

Fighting an overwhelming urge to pass out, Dolan worked his hand against the force of the current to a latch on the upper right hand side of the grate. The latch was a simple clamp that kept the grate from swinging outwards with the force of the water. Fumbling blindly, Dolan wrapped and rewrapped his fingers around the latch slowly working it out of its socket. Gritting his teeth, Dolan inched his way closer to the latch to get a better grip. Water and gunk still roared past his body and dropped into the river below. Closer now, Dolan could see a bit more clearly what was happening. Grasping the rebar tightly in his left hand, he pulled on the latch with his right—

Smack! Whoosh! Crack! As the latch came free, Dolan and the metal grate were thrown outward into the afternoon air.

Water rushed past and fell freely into the river below. Hanging by one hand, Dolan dangled from the grate. Water continued to batter into him leaving him gasping for breath as the grate swung back and forth above the falling water. He couldn't fight against the onslaught for long. Already his arm was tiring. Dolan looked down through the water to the river below. The thirty foot dropped now seemed more like one hundred. He grimaced as his ankle dangled uselessly from his leg and fought against the panic that threatened to overtake his brain.

The sewer drainage tunnel where he came out was enclosed in cement. The cement surrounded the tunnel opening and sloped downwards at a steep angle into the river. The concrete form was discoloured and slimy from years of runoff passing over it. When there was heavy flow, there was a waterfall. When the flow was light, the water merely trickled down the steep slope and into the river. Below was the river silently carving its lazy course through the city valley.

Dolan squinted and blinked as the shining sun contracted his pupils. He quickly surveyed his surroundings. His fatigued, adrenaline-overdosed body continued to hang, dripping and swaying from the grate.

He had no choice. He couldn't swing back into the tunnel with all the sewer water running out. He also couldn't hold on forever. He would have to drop and do his best to avoid the waterfall driving him into the river floor.

This was going to hurt.

Closing his eyes, and mustering courage—Dolan took a deep breath. He felt his numb fingers begin to slip. His body's instinct was to crawl and hide, but that was not an option.

*This is it*, he thought.

Throwing all his weight forward, Dolan swung his legs up and out and released at the apex of his swing. His momentum carried him forward, but not far enough. Tonnes of water smashed unforgivingly into the back of his shoulders driving every molecule of air from his lungs.

The fall was quick.

Barely able to grasp a breath, Dolan felt his body smash into the river and submerge. Excruciating pain stabbed like knives through his legs as they tried to cushion his fall. Pain from his ankle buckling underneath him as he hit the bottom of the river sent another wave of torment through his body. Silver, previously clinging to his clothing was scattered into the river and the pounding water peeled any remainder of the slime from his body. Holding his breath and forcing his body to relax, he let the current carry him around the falls and into open water. Dolan sputtered to the surface for air and manoeuvred himself into a back float. He tried to flutter kick and immediately regretted the action. Crying out in anger more than pain, tears burned his eyes and he squeezed them shut until the piercing pain dulled to a throb.

Dolan forced his body to relax and with the adrenaline and energy that is reserved solely for life and death situations, he began to hand paddle his limp, tired, and aching body to the opposite shore.

\* \* \*

Brandon used his long arms to keep himself bouncing from one side of the tunnel to the other. His red hair floated in the dark waters, pushed back and forth as the water passed through it. His pants and clothing sagged from the weight of the water, and his eyes beamed silver rays into the sewer tunnels, Silently, he moved through the tunnels as the waters willed.

Subtly, Brandon felt a slight change in the currents and depth of water. The water's rage seemed to have abated. The currents grew weaker and Brandon stood up. The murky water created dread-like clumps with his hair while driblets of mud ran like black tears from his glowing eyes. Brandon opened his mouth to breathe. A cool lump of Silver was climbing up his throat. He gagged and retched until the substance filled his mouth and lathered his tongue. It seemed to whisper something to him, but then it spilled over his bottom lip and dripped off his chin into his waiting hand. Brandon straightened and dry heaved a large gob of mucousy spit into the water.

Suddenly, a sharp light pierced his vision. Every nerve ending screamed, every cone burned as the silver saviour pulled itself from his eyes. Like tears of mercury, it rolled down his cheeks and within seconds, they too had dropped into the palm of his hands.

A feeling of emptiness lingered inside. A vacuum.

He looked at the Silver in his hands, "Thank you," he whispered. A voice whispered back. Faint. Brandon paused unsure of what he heard. Shaking his head, he turned his hand upside down to let the Silver run off his palms and into the water. Instead, it clung. Swirling, and glowing but not leaving. Brandon turned his hand right side up.

"You want to stay with me, don't you?" he murmured. Slipping the Silver into his drenched shirt pocket, Brandon hiked up his pants, and shivering continued to walk and swim in the direction the water was taking him.

Brandon rounded a corner of the tunnel and was immediately blinded by sunlight. Relief flooded his entire body. Quickening his steps, he arrived at the mouth of the sewage system. Now only thigh high in water, he paused and let the sun begin to warm his face. Brandon looked around slowly assessing his situation.

A large fall, slick cement, falling water, a steel grated doorway and the river below . . . the options were quite limited. Peeling off his filthy jeans, Brandon reached for the grate, pulled it in, and tied a pant leg to it. He pulled. It held firm. He struggled out of his shirt, tied it to the pant leg, and pulled again. It held firm. Inching forward, shirt in hand, Brandon looked out to the river and silently reviewed his plan:

*if I can slip down even 4 ft this will lessen the impact of my fall . . . I could brace my legs against the slippery cement and push off . . . hopefully to land in the river a couple feet ahead of the pounding water . . .* with clammy hands, shivering in his white underwear, Brandon lowered himself down.

\*　　\*　　\*

After dragging himself to shore, Dolan pulled his body up onto the sun-warmed rocks. He lay exhausted. He heard a soft ticking noise and looked up. It was a bicycle. He squinted and looked again. It was an RCMP officer riding a bike—one of the ones who patrolled the bike paths. The officer knelt down beside him, adjusted his belt and took his wrist as he felt for a pulse. Just before he passed out, Dolan heard the officer make a call.

"MB16 to dispatch".

"Go ahead MB16"

"I'm 50m east of the trestle bridge in Lower Fairview. South side. I have an 8-37 here. He's a native male, approximately 15 years old, broken ankle, unconscious but breathing. Send EMS.

"Copy that. EMS on the way."

"10-4."

\*　　\*　　\*

Hanging onto his shirt, Brandon watched the waterfall in front of him. He would need to push hard to break through. Slapping his feet against the wall, Brandon tried to brace himself. Feeling around with his feet, his shoes caught a chip in the cement. Desperately ramming his toe into the only hold, he readied himself. With a grunt, Brandon pushed off past the stream of water, into the afternoon air and at the apex let go. He fell. With a loud splash, the river accepted its second visitor that day. Brandon sunk to the bottom of the river, and forced his way upwards as soon as he touched bottom. After breaking through, he gasped for breath, red hair clinging to the sides of his face. He looked back at the tunnel.

A glint of silver sparkled off the walls inside. His clothes dangled from the grate like a forlorn flag.

"I'll be back . . ." he whispered, "Thank you." Treading water and kicking softly he let the current pull him to the river's edge.

Brandon saw an ambulance on the other side of the river, but preoccupied with being almost naked, he sneaked into the bushes and took off without a second glance.

\*     \*     \*

Back in the tunnel a series of impulses were sent through the darkness. The silver globs glowed brightly as the impulse passed through them.

*We let him go.*

*He'll be back.*

*We should've taken him.*

*It's not our nature.*

*We need him.*

*He'll be back.*

*We need him.*

*We still have him.*

# Chapter Eleven

June 23<sup>rd</sup>
6 days later

Friday night again. Keenan and Carlee conversed softly in their shared room. It was going to be a long night. Mom started drinking at four o'clock. Friends had been arriving since five o'clock. Lights on, huddled together in the bedroom corner, they sat and prayed silently no one would know they were there.

\*     \*     \*

Outside their room, down the hall, into the kitchen and out the front door, Tyler sat languidly on the worn, white deck. The deck was narrow and stretched the length of the front of the house. Sitting in a chair, Tyler could lean back against the house and have his feet up on the railing. Feet up, smoking, a beer in his left hand, he waited for his 'girlfriend' Crystil to show up. Crystil was hot. Turning, Tyler watched his mom, also sitting on the deck. She tilted her head back and her black hair brushed the worn wooden siding of the house. She downed her beer.

"Friday night, eh?" Tyler looked out to the street again.

"Oh yeah . . ."

Tyler blew out his smoke into the air above him, "How's Dolan feeling?"

"You know Dolan. He's been caught twice already by security guards racing wheel chairs down the hallways."

"You think he'll be . . . Ok?"

"Of course," Lori stretched and looked past the deck and down the street.

"I mean," Tyler gestured with a twirling finger at this temple, "O.K?"

Silence. Her mind wondered the same thing. All this stuff about glowing Silver was a bit farfetched. Lori continued to stare. Tyler watched her push her glasses up on her nose and finger the acne pock marks on her cheeks.

Tyler pushed further, "The whole silver stuff saving him . . . you know . . . do you think he's lying."

"Dolan doesn't lie to his mother." With that, Lori looked sharply at him and headed back into the house.

A long inhale. Hold. A long exhale. "The bugger's lying," he stated to himself, "the little freeloading bugger is lying."

\*      \*      \*

Cheers, loud noises, the sound of glass smashing, drunken laughter—this was the worst sound. To Keenan's ears it sounded like the devil. The obnoxious chortle, followed by a swig, and a gurgled laugh as another house item or person was smashed. Arms wrapped around his legs, he rocked back and forth in the closet, as he tried to wait out the storm. Carlee sat close by, engaged in a magazine, but wary none the less.

As the night wore on, Keenan's stomach began to rumble. It was all he could think about. He was hungry. Getting up slowly and stretching out his cramps, he stepped gingerly to the door.

Listening to the sounds of the party, he opened the door and headed precariously down the hallway to the kitchen. Stopping to wipe crumbs off the bottom of his feet, he glanced around the corner at the party unfolding in the house. Quickly and avoiding all eye contact, he walked along the worn cupboards to the small pantry in the corner. Bending low, he opened the door and looked inside for what was edible.

Wham. Wham.

The sound shocked Keenan and he swung his head around to see where the noise came from.

His arms began to shake.

"Well now, who do we have here? Stealing food from your mother and me, eh you little rat."

"I-I'm not stealing," Keenan's voice squeaked a little. He quickly averted his eyes.

Brad stood at the counter some three feet from Keenan. He had a beer in his hand, and his eyes had the wild, intoxicated look. Brad was short for a grown man, 5'8". He was however, stocky. His blond scraggly hair hung limply over his ears. He always wore the same jeans, bleached ones that he never washed. His tight black t-shirt stretched over his meaty frame. Keenan lived in perpetual fear of Brad and for good reason. Brad, in his effort to find control in his alcohol-induced life, physically picked on Keenan. This often resulted in bruises and bloody urine from sore kidneys.

Keenan was constantly fighting for some element of control in his life too. Brad's presence left him constantly cowering in fear. Keenan was struggling for control at this moment—a figh between a physical need for nourishment and a very physical ne· for safety.

Glazed eyes now stared at Keenan in the dingy kitchen light. A dirty sink, once stainless steel, but now grimy brown, supported Keenan as he inched away from the menace. Brad glared evilly.

"Why don't you let us party without you stealing from us, you filthy brat!" he bellowed at Keenan. A few adults looked up vaguely from the couch.

Stumbling backwards past the cupboards and against the hallway wall, Keenan struggled to control his panic so he could think of a way out. Brad took a step closer and grabbed for Keenan's neck. Keenan dropped down and dove between Brad's legs. Brad, turned around in anger bellowing like an enraged bull.

"Come here you scum and say you're sorry!"

Keenan ran quickly into his and Carlee's room, slammed the door and locked it. Carlee quickly jumped up and helped Keenan move the mattress up against the door.

Brad began to pound on the door and yell. Keenan, tears streaming down his face, continued to pile more stuff against the door. He began to shake. Wringing his hands, and pacing across the room, his breathing became more panicked.

"Keenan," Carlee said softly, "The pounding has stopped. I think Brad is gone now." Keenan, still crying, continued to pace.

"I can't stay here Carlee. I hate him. I hate him so much." He was close to blubbering now. Carlee stepped up and grabbed Keenan's hands. Keenan stopped. She held them, and drew him near. "I know enan, I know. We're safe . . . for now." She reached up and wiped ears off his cheek. "I'm so sorry Keenan. I'm so sorry."

nan looked up. Red rimmed eyes looked into red rimmed eyes. anding passed between them. Keenan pulled her close and they ke down. Her tears mixed with his as she held him tight. Keenan

trembled as he fought to gain control of himself. Carlee gently stroked
his hair while he cried. Together, Keenan and Carlee crouched in the
corner. Together, in that corner something changed. Together, silently
they both knew that somehow their lives would have to change.

\*     \*     \*

Dolan hobbled down the hallways on his crutches. Hospitals
weren't really his thing. They smelled stale, the food was stale and
the people were stale. Time to cut loose.

After signing out for a walk at the nursing station, he turned left
down the main hallway towards the elevators. What was up with these
doctors anyways? *Why do I need a CAT scan?* I broke my stinkin' ankle.
Why all the attention and the looks? At first Dolan enjoyed the excessive
amount of attention he received. However, it was day three now and
enough was enough. *Maybe it's my good looks*, Dolan thought. I *am rather
stunning, if I do say so myself.* With a smile, and confident hobble, Dolan
headed to the where the laundry was waiting. He grabbed his folded,
clean clothes from the pile, and after quickly changing in the bathroom,
descended to the main floor and hobbled out the front doors. With no
agenda for the day, he took off north to his mother's house.

\*     \*     \*

June 23rd
Sunday, late afternoon

Brandon wandered around downtown. Brick buildings lined
the streets. Looking down alleyways he could see graffiti sprayed

nonsensically (to his untrained eye) across a back door in an enclosed stairwell.

"Why bother," he wondered. "What's the use if no one can read it or even see it."

Sauntering across the road, he stopped at the other side and looked into the barred window of the gaming shop.

*Why is everything closed on Sunday?* He thought. *Sheesh.*

He looked at his reflection in the window. The clothes he picked out were his own—though he hated the pants he picked. They were corduroy and made him feel like a little kid.

Brandon thought again about going home to see his mom. The first time he had been careful. He had ducked in, grabbed some food and clothes and ducked out again. Why? In the sewer, all he wanted was to be home again. Now that the opportunity presented itself, he was reluctant. That was six days ago and he still hadn't gone home. He was sure his mother was desperate and the cops were looking for him. He didn't care. His longing to go home was diminished.

Sunken. Irrelevant.

Brandon sat on the edge of the curb on the empty street. His mind turned over the events of the last few days . . .

*He had arrived home in his underwear and immediately realized his mom was gone. The house was in disarray as usual, and there was an ashtray full of cigarettes on the table. There was no note to him, no sign of anyone missing him. Not that he knew what that sign might look like, or what it was that he expected . . . nonetheless, he felt . . . disappointed. He hadn't seen hide nor hair of Dolan and Brooks and frankly didn't care. They had deserted him down in the tunnels. The stupid jerks.*

*There was a new friend now. A silver one. The thought of the glowing slime brought an aching and a longing. He wanted to feel its coolness again. He felt so . . . so powerful in the tunnels. He wanted it back.*

*He wrote a note to his mother explaining that he was fine and not to worry. He quickly dashed out of the house after getting some clothing and food and headed back downtown.*

The rest was kind of a blur. His body fought with his mind as he wandered through the city. There were cravings he did not understand, there were voices in his mind trying to tell him something. At times, they were strong, and at other times, they were distant. Confused, Brandon struggled to make sense of what was happening inside of himself.

Today was the sixth day and the restlessness still brewed deep within.

Standing up, Brandon turned to walk across the street, and a glint of light flitted across his peripheral vision. Brandon turned left, glanced up and down and then quickly looked around again to see if anyone saw him. Nobody around. The core of downtown was usually dead on early Sunday evening. Forcing his thoughts outward, he turned to walk back across the street.

Again, a stab of light lightly struck his peripheral vision. Again, Brandon paused and looked around.

No one. No one, but maybe something. Brandon stood stalk still in the middle of the empty downtown street. The sun flitted through the buildings casting long shadows across the black tarmac. The windows of the used games store were a mirror casting a stunning yellow glow over his clothes. Brandon stood . . . pausing . . . pausing . . . waiting . . . the flash of light would come again. He was sure. He felt a tingle, as the adrenaline in his veins began to increase. Something was happening.

A flash.

From below. It wasn't a reflection. Brandon crouched closer to the road and waited.

Again, the sparkle of light. Stronger this time. He crawled, hands and knees on the pavement, oblivious to his surroundings. Again he waited.

Brandon became more aware. Aware that his blood was pulsating and beating at his temples and that the tips of his fingers had begun to burn. His own blood began to . . . almost . . . silently urge him towards the manhole. With trembling hands and heart, Brandon inched his way towards the iron grate nestled in the alleyway. The grate was sunken into the cement close to the buildings lining the alley. His restlessness turning to anticipation he . . .

Flash.

Brandon peered down into the familiar blackness.

Flash.

Blood pounding now, eyes focused, Brandon reached his fingers into the space below. A cool feeling washed over his fingers and began crawl up his arm. Relief washed over him.

Excitement. Rapture. Longing.

Brandon relaxed and let the familiar coolness soothe the craving his body had been feeling. The restlessness subsided. The silver ooze climbed up his arm, his neck and searched out his eyes. With a gasp, Brandon threw his head back as a burning flash of light drowned his vision. He arched his back, clenched his fist and welcomed the intrusion.

# Chapter Twelve

June 23<sup>rd</sup>
late Sunday afternoon

Kendra arrived home from work, kicked off her work shoes and slumped into the chair at the kitchen table. Looking around at the pile of dishes in the sink and jam spilt on the counter caused her to droop a bit more. She was tired. Tired of having to work all day and then having to come home and work some more. She had just finished a weekend shift at the group home. Once a month, she had to spend the whole weekend at the home looking after three men with mental health issues. These weekends always taxed her patience. By the time it was Sunday afternoon she was ready to leave. The men were as frustrated with her as she was with them. Hooking her foot under a nearby chair, she dragged it closer and put her feet up. Kendra lifted her rough, bleach-smelling hands to her face. Putting her back against the chair, she sighed, and thought about going to go shower. Her eyes fell on a hand written note. Kendra casually picked up the paper, noting the writing was from her only son Brandon, read it quickly and tossed it back on the table. *He's probably at Dolan's again,* she thought, *that's where he always seems to hang out these days.*

\*    \*    \*

Walking along the riverside, Keenan and Carlee each silently munched their half of a burger.

"Let's stop here," Keenan said with a mouthful. He pointed to a place where they could watch the water gushing out of the sewer system. As they finished their lunch, the two sat adjacent to the cement scaffold and watched the water pour into the river beside them. The waterfall created a mist and the grass surrounding the area was a deep green. They stood to walk down the steep bank to the river's edge. They had to put their hands up against the cliff as they slipped and stepped to the bottom. At the river, large flat stones boarded the edge providing great places to cast fishing line. Keenan and Carlee jumped along the rocks looking in the water for the glint of discarded or lost fishhooks. Taking off their shoes and socks, and rolling up their pant legs, they let their feet soak in the cool river.

"I love how the water sparkles in the sun," whispered Carlee, "It's like . . . like there are silver jewels in the river."

"Yeah, every time you needed money you could just jump in the river and get some, eh?" answered Keenan.

"Yeah. We could be rich."

"Yeah."

Together they watched the water, the river, the sun . . . the glint off the water . . . the silver glittering . . .

"I really feel like I could grab that silver you know."

"I know what you mean . . . I'm feeling the same way . . . sorta," replied Carlee.

"Weird, huh?"

Carlee nodded absently.

Things got quiet between them. The water became background noise, the sun grew hot, and hunger was staved. Carlee withdrew her feet and stepped cautiously back to where the grass was growing. Curling up, she laid down on the grass.

Keenan got up and walked to the river's edge. Picking up a few rocks, he skipped them into the water. Rinsing his hands, he rubbed some of the cold river water on his face.

"I'm boiling hot," Keenan announced. He looked back at his twin sister for a response.

Carlee merely muttered . . . something . . . and drifted off to sleep.

Sun bounced off the water drops and streamed down his face. Keenan blinked out the drops and rubbed his eyes with his hands. Glancing at his fingers, he took notice of a smeared silver substance. Quickly wiping his hands on his pants, Keenan hopped to where Carlee was laying, curled up beside her and let the heat of the sun woo him to sleep also.

\*     \*     \*

Colors radiated from every light source. The spectrum refracted continually casting green, purple, yellow, rose hues over everything. Brandon sat down and let the light show dazzle and dance before him. I'm in Heaven he thought. He lifted his hand to his face. His thumbnail glowed; the edges of it shooting out Silver spears of light. Brandon slowly brought his tongue to his thumb. Cold spread over his tongue heightening the savage taste of his rotten breath in his mouth. Brandon gagged and spat. He could taste the stale, filmy sugar paste of the cookies he had eaten last. Brandon gagged again as the individual tastes of more recently eaten foods also bombarded his taste buds. Shaking it off, Brandon reached into the manhole and pulled out even more Silver. This time Brandon lathered his hands and arms and paused to allow the ionic substance to soak into this skin like hand lotion.

As the coolness began to subside, Brandon stood up and looked for something to touch. The ground, the metal manhole cover, a cigarette butt, a brick wall, a tree . . . a tree . . . Brandon walked to the tree, reached up and grabbed a leaf still hanging from the branch. Closing his eyes he rubbed the leaf in between his fingers. He could feel every tiny cilia hair on the leaf and caressed them softly. He pressed harder and became aware of the tiny pulse of phloem traveling through the veins of the leaf. Pressing firmer yet again, he could feel a thousand pulsating bumps massaging his fingertips. The beating nuclei of each cell beat out a response to his touch.

Opening his eyes, Brandon gasped as he saw only a normal leaf between his fingers. He popped the leaf from the tree, and placed it in his pocket. *I need more*, Brandon thought. Ravenous now, he locked his fingers around the manhole grates and heaved. Nothing. Not even a budge. Brandon looked at his biceps. Scrawny. He would never be able to move this grate—he would need a crowbar for some leverage. Looking down at his hands, there was a slight sheen, a soft glow emanating just beneath the cover. Brandon reached his fingers again in through the grate hole and scraped off the last bit of Silver clinging to the sides. He smeared it into the palms of his hands. Breathing heavy with anticipation, Brandon placed both hands on the metal grate and squeezed hard.

At first, there was no give. But then the texture of the metal began to change. It seemed to melt in his hands and become squishy. He let go. The metal hardened leaving hand and finger indentations in its form. Unbelievable.

Brandon, mind sparking with potential ideas, grabbed the grate with both hands and squeezed. The metal broke free from the grate and he was holding jagged chunks in his hand. He threw them off to the side and grabbed the next bar and again squeezed. The metal, hard at first, squished in his hands like play-dough until it gave way. These ones he dropped down into the sewer. Brandon did the same to the last two bars across the grate. There was now enough room for him to squeeze in and drop into the tunnels . . . again.

Brandon, squeezed his body through the jagged hole until he was hanging onto the edge of the grate with his feet dangling into the blackness.

*     *     *

As the sun sunk in the sky, shadows crept their way along the sleeping duo. The warmth of the sun became replaced by the slight chill. Carlee shivered, sat up and placed a hand on Keenan.

"Keenan," she whispered, "We need to get going."

Keenan roused himself and looked at Carlee. The sun was behind her casting rainbows around her head. Keenan blinked again. And again. The colors of the world around began to blur and then quickly his vision sharpened. Pulling his eyes from Carlee he looked to the river bed and rubbed the sleep from his eyes. Keenan pulled his knees up to his chest and hugged them. The river was fairly calm and so was his stomach. His eyes caressed the bank of the river and landed on the pebbly shore.

"Look at that bug!" he laughed and jumped down to the muddy edge.

"What bug?" called Carlee after him.

Reaching down, Keenan picked up a small beetle with a gold back. The beetle crawled along his hand. Keenan turned his hand over and let the beetle crawl on the other side. Gently, he picked up the beetle between his two fingers and placed it in a tree.

Smiling he walked back up by Carlee.

"What was that all about?" asked Carlee.

"The beetle, it was going to drown."

"Huh?"

"The beetle—the black one with the gold back—it was going to drown."

Keenan watched the beetle as it scuttled up the tree and disappeared into the leaves. Carlee watched Keenan watch the beetle and shook her head. *That was weird,* she thought.

\*     \*     \*

Despite the blackness, Brandon could see. Years of old muck clung to the walls. The musty, slightly rancid smell was familiar. The memories of rushing helplessly through the tunnels bombarded his brain as he dropped with a splash into the ankle high sewer water. Brandon could sense the tunnels come alive with his presence. As a host to the Silver pulsing through him, he was like a magnet to the other globs stuck on the walls. He knelt down and picked up a chunk of metal from the grate. Turning it over in his hands, he scoffed at it.

"I'm stronger than steel!"

Raising his arm, he threw the hunk of metal into the blackness. It bounced off the wall and splashed into the water. He moved forward. Each glob of the Silver glowed brightly as he neared, but then dimmed as he passed.

Brandon's brain was hyper-sensitive and sharp. Thoughts, ideas, equations blasted in and out of his mind like the turn wheel at his mother's bingo hall. He stopped and basked for a moment in the sensations bombarding his body. Looking down at his hands and how they glowed, he began instinctively to rub them together. Silver gathered together ready to obey his every command. Brandon smiled.

Then, a thought stopped him short . . . Where am I going?

More thoughts floated to the surface, Should I go any further? Where will I stay? Can I go back outside like this? I have to hide.

His thoughts were immediately complimented by a series of answers that were persistent and yet whispered gently.

*Move forward.*

*Don't stop.*

*Listen.*

*We'll direct you.*

*Gather us.*

*Keep moving.*

Brandon shook his head to clear the voices. They only continued.

*There is a safe place.*

*Find the source.*

*The source needs you.*

*We need you.*

Brandon's eyes glowed and he understood. This was his destiny. This was a spirit talking to him. Putting his hands in his pocket, he continued to follow the whispered directions.

\*   \*   \*

Dolan stared across the river at the water splashing out of the sewer tunnel. He was headed home on the bus, but felt instinctively drawn here. Spontaneously, he pulled the line at the Lower Fairview bus stop and hobbled down to the river's edge. Sitting, leg hoisted up on a rock, he gazed across the river. A steady stream of water pushed through the rusted grate. It was still unfastened and swinging back and forth as the water hit it. There were clothes hanging from it.

Weird. How did someone get up there to tie clothes on it?

The placid river ran softly over rocks, causing the riverweed to sway slightly back and forth. A young couple, probably in love, lay resting or sleeping to the right of the waterfall. The sunlight glazing off the water made Dolan squint his eyes. Thousands of sparkles, like hundreds of diamonds reflected off the water. Dolan soaked it all in . . . relaxing . . . remembering . . . then something caught his eye . . . something wasn't right. Some of the sparkles were refracting rainbows and others weren't. Odd. Dolan moved his body.

It must be the angle, he thought.

Again, rainbows and just silver. Silver? Abruptly, he understood. He knew what they were. They had saved his life.

Dolan struggled up, gave a last glance at the river and its Silver, and headed back up to the bike path to the nearest bridge.

*     *     *

June 24<sup>th</sup>
Monday Morning

"Can you wipe the dust off the board, Ms. Shalby?"

"What dust Keenan? I'm sure everything is fine."

"Seriously, the dust on the board is making it hard to read." Ms. Shalby, the school art specialist, looked at Keenan disconcertingly, trying to figure out if he was serious or not. This definitely was not like him at all.

With that, Keenan got up, went to the board, and using his shirtsleeve, he wiped a fine layer of dust off. Lifting up his arm to show Ms. Shalby the dust residue, and sat back down. Somewhat stunned, Ms. Shalby continued teaching the class.

# Chapter Thirteen

June 24<sup>th</sup>

$B$randon continued slogging his way through the tunnels in a trance-like state. He didn't know where he was going . . . he just listened to the voices. Turn after turn. Deeper. Sometimes sliding, sometimes skidding, but always deeper.

The stale air began to get warmer. Brandon was sweating profusely now. His shirt and pants clung to him and his breath became laboured. Still the voices sang. The song was beautiful. The chorus was rich, full, gentle and soothing.

*Don't stop.*

*Find the source.*

*Move, always move.*

*The source needs you.*

*Don't stop.*

Brandon looked around. The tunnels were smaller down here. His head almost touched the top. The sludge around his feet was mostly dried up now, which made walking easier. Disturbed and puzzled, he noticed that the tunnels seemed to be getting brighter rather than darker.

"Where am I?" The echo of his own voice startled and alarmed him. Fear. It pierced like a knife through the coagulation of Silver webbed voices. The whispers scattered.

"I'm lost again." He spoke louder this time. "I'm lost!"

Panic-stricken, Brandon turned round and around.

Momentarily disorganized, the Silver clambered over one another to be heard. The noise buzzed around him like a hive of bees.

Brandon looked around in the lighted tunnel. How did he get here? What was he doing down here again?

He stayed motionless, looking at the curved tunnel walls, now pulsating with the Silver. Captivating. He stared in wonder. Captive.

Tempted to give in to the voices, Brandon stood rigidly. His brain battled for control over his body.

*You want us.*

*You need us.*

*Take us.*

*Take us into you.*

The whispers were stronger now. One strong voice, a thousand whispers in unison.

Brandon's body began to ache. His muscles were sore, his feet swollen, his mouth dry. He imagined how refreshing the Silver would feel on his skin and inside his body.

I want it.

Still Brandon didn't move. The connection he had with the Silver, momentarily severed by the knife of fear, became re-established. Brandon's senses overtook his reason. Without conscious thought he reached out and gingerly touched the tunnel wall. Immediately, relief flooded up his hand and arm. Powerful. More potent than ever before.

The walls rippled as the Silver moved towards him. He could feel the ionic power in the room aching to be a part of him. Brandon lifted his hands slowly away from the cement snapping the Silver back against the wall.

Curiosity emerged and was now partitioning a barrier in his mind. The persistent voices began to fade. "Where is all this Silver coming from? Why the high concentration of it here?" he wondered aloud.

Brandon's gaze was drawn further down the ever-brightening tunnel. There. There will be the answer to my questions. Ducking his head slightly, Brandon continued forward.

Silver continued to pulse and ripple as he passed. Ions raced along the gelatinous fluid following his path and lighting his way.

Ducking, then hunching and eventually crawling, Brandon continued on. Abruptly, the tunnel ended on the edge of a small precipice. Lying on his belly now, Brandon peered curiously over the edge. Bright light accosted his vision. Impulsively closing his eyes he grabbed handfuls of the Silver which now totally surrounded him and lathered it over them. Instantly, the voices returned.

*Take the source.*

*Look.*

*See.*

*Touch.*

*Feel.*

*Become.*

Peering through the translucent jelly dripping from his eye sockets, he looked out again.

Below him, about a 50cm away, was a blazing ball of Silver. Tendrils of the ooze left the ball, streaming up the walls like vines on an old English mansion. The kaleidoscope of colors was mesmerizing. Silvers—shooting, swishing, gurgling, flinging, splashing, crawling, sizzling. Alive. The voices, buzzing, began again to join as one. Beautifully and intricately the voices began to weave together. They bounced octaves and slid scales and meshed into one harmonic and soothing voice—

*Touch Me.*

Brandon, now completely under the spell of the Silver orb, gave up his struggle, his curiosity. Reaching forward and then down over the edge, he brought both hands to hover over the pulsating mass.

*Touch Me.*

Brandon stretched forward some more and placed his hands onto the glowing mass. Coolness, frighteningly alive, oozed around his fingers. Brandon could feel the power in the room and sensed its excitement. This was the source. Brandon, now completely entranced, edged back holding the blazing ball.

*Take me.*

Silver was now dripping all over his hands and arms. Brandon, on his stomach, held the orb in front of his face.

*I am yours.*

The orb grew brighter in anticipation. Silver tendrils reached out, caressed his face, and slithered over his body. Brandon's whole body felt awake. A fleeting thought—*will I regret this*—was quickly silenced. Lifting the orb closer, Brandon opened his mouth wide and inhaled the force into his body.

The shock of the foreign intruder rocked his brain. His eyes shut and Brandon bathed in a temporary ecstasy before sliding into a state of unconsciousness.

The source had claimed its host.

# PART II

*A New Host*

# Chapter Fourteen

*Red Deer Advocate*                                    Date: Monday, July 7th

Apparition emerges

Residents of Central Alberta's major city are thinking of actually leaving their prosperous homeland. Folks are preparing to pack up and leave due to the alleged appearance of a ghost wandering the downtown core at night.

"I won't raise my children where ghosts haunt the streets," stated one woman while packing up her apartment.

Others are not so sure about leaving, but are definitely 'keeping their eyes peeled'.

Ms. Flannigan, a downtown business owner states, "I have heard noises and read the stories, but I'm not prepared to pack up and leave. I have too much invested in this community."

Lindsay Osban, a downtown outreach worker, states adamantly that the apparition approached her own soup bus asking for food. "When the ghost approached the bus, I immediately slammed the door and drove away. I looked back but the apparition had disappeared."

Lindsay describes the ghost as fearful looking with glowing eyes and a glowing body. This description is similar to other reports that also identify a frightening male with glowing eyes. Some even say this ghost passes through walls, climbs buildings, and hovers in the air.

Is the apparition, the ghost-friendly? Is it merely hungry? Why is it downtown? What does it want? Should we be watching our children more closely? Are the stories based on fact or do we have sensationalized reports made by over-sensitive, frightened people?

Dr. Crawham, a noted psychologist, stated that "People will often see things that are not really there if they are in a high stress situation or taking certain substances."

Our Chief of police, Rock ruther, was unavailable for comment.

Judge for yourself. Keep your eyes peeled for the glowing ghost especially in the evening.

If you spot the glowing ghost, report it to Cindy Stoffers at 343-0845.

"**W**eird, eh?" Tyler said as he threw the paper on the coffee table. Keenan watched dust fly up into the air and float in the evening sunbeams.

"I wish they had a photograph."

"Yeah," Tyler replied, "Then we'd know if the ghost is really real."

"I think he's real," Carlee added . . .

"Yeah, he'll hunt us in our sleep and suck our blood!"

"Shut up!" Carlee jumped up and began punching Tyler. Tyler, laughing, defended himself. "Ok, Ok—the glowing ghost won't come and suck your blood. Instead, he'll send out energy waves that will control your mind and then he'll take over your body and use you to commit crimes."

Carlee climbed off Tyler and stood on the floor. "Do you think that?"

Tyler looked up at her amused, "Yes. And I think the glowing ghost has many friends as well that slowly want to take everyone over and then use our brains for soup!" He began to laugh at his own joke.

Carlee smiled. "You're a jerk sometimes you know."

"Thanks sis. I love you too."

Keenan sat and watched the playful interaction, his imagination already dreaming what things would be like if what his brother said actually happened.

He had no idea that his dreams were about to become a reality.

\* \* \*

Cloaked in vapour, silver swirling and dancing around him, Brandon peered into the window of the City Bank downtown. It was dark outside. The streetlights provided only a dim light. Brandon ran his hands over his face as he looked at his own cloudy reflection. He looked at his hands. They were alive with Silver. He clapped them together and closed his eyes. Silver swarmed down his arms and into a small puddle in his hands. He smiled. Over the past two weeks, Brandon had experienced the power that accompanied the ability to control. Control came easily *if* you could frighten people. Fear allowed him to dominate others. He could eat, play and use as he wished. Brandon opened his eyes to his reflection once more. Tonight was time to play. The Silver had directed him here to this bank. So here he was.

Other nights were different. There were times when the Silver just let him experiment with his new powers and experiment he did. He had feasted on junk food, scared homeless people and practiced aiming the Silver at objects. A couple times he had stepped out to address someone he knew and then stopped. He was different now. An outcast. Feared. This was disorienting at first, disconcerting and even lonely—but he had pulled through. With his newfound abilities, Brandon found he could easily put his feelings aside as he scoured the city at night feasting, playing and exploring.

During the day, Brandon made his way back into the sewers and slept. Tonight he was at the bank. From the moment he woke up, he had sensed a seriousness about this mission that he didn't fully understand. The usual 'tingle of excitement' he would feel from the voices was not there. Instead, there was a sense of urgency. The voices demanded; the impulses almost aggressive.

Brandon peered at his reflection again. He noticed that his freckles seemed to glow more brightly than his skin. His thoughts drifted back to the years of insults from the kids at school. Everything from 'Alphabet soup' to 'Carrot brains' had been thrown at him. *I wonder what they would say if they could see me now?* He smiled as he imagined the look on his schoolmates faces as he walked into the classroom.

Brandon broke away from the window, looked once more up the street and began. He ran his hands down his glowing body. The source, now inside of him, pumped Silver through his veins. Although he couldn't see it, the source had settled under his skin and coated his heart. Its chilling coolness was a constant reminder of its presence. The Silver constantly reproduced itself so the power was always there. No matter how much Silver Brandon used to accomplish a deed, there was still more for him to use.

He lathered up two fistfuls of the swirling, molten gel, rubbed them together, and moulded them into a singular Silver point. Brandon and the Silver worked as one—sharing thoughts and ideas. Within minutes, Brandon was brandishing a glowing blade. Pressing its fine edge against the glass pane, he slowly drew it down. At the blade's touch, the glass split and spliced . . . another line at a right angle and then two more. The glass fell inward with a smash. The sound was stark and loud in the quiet night. Brandon allowed the knife to dissolve into a puddle into his hands, and stepped into the bank.

The motion detector began to beep a warning signal. He had to disarm it now, or the security police would come running. Brandon rolled the Silver into a ball in his hands. He looked up into the corner where the detector was beeping and hurled the Silver into the room. The slime flew through the air, straight and true and slathered the motion detector. Immediately, the Silver melded into the system and rendered the alarm useless.

Stepping confidently into the foyer of the bank, Brandon made his way behind the counters. The Silver's whispers led him to a door, which led into the back of the bank and down a hallway. Brandon tested the latch. It was locked. Brandon stepped back and simply tossed a ball of Silver into the door. The door splintered, leaving a large jagged hole. Brandon stepped through and continued down the dark hallway. The light from the emergency exit signs, and his own silver glow, let Brandon see easily as he made his way to the elevator at the end. Here, Brandon paused and listened. The Silver continued giving directions and Brandon pushed the button to descend into the basement of the bank. A yellow sign with bright red words warned— AUTHORIZED PERSONELONLY and hung above the elevator.

The doors opened with a whirr and he stepped inside. Looking at the number pad, he wondered which button to push. *Down*. Brandon obeyed. He began by pushing the B1 button. As the elevator whirred and began its descent, Brandon stood still, his eyes blank as he focussed inward so he could hear the persistent directions.

Ding.

The door opened on what was presumably the B1 floor. No good, just another hallway of offices. *Lower.*

Brandon pushed the button for B2. Again the descent.

Ding.

The door opened into a darkened, carpeted hallway. Brandon kept one hand on the door and stepped onto the worn red carpet. He hesitated and stepped back into the elevator. The door whirred shut. There were no more buttons and no more floors. Brandon listened.

*There is another floor. We feel it.*

*Find it.*

Brandon ran his hands down the panel, not really sure what he was looking for. He caressed the edges—nothing unusual. Kneeling down, he began to knock on the walls. He listened for something—perhaps a hollow space. He began at the bottom and worked his way up and around the elevator. The panelling on the elevator walls gave a muffled 'umph' as he knocked on them. Then, as he came around to the back of the elevator, the sound changed. He moved upwards, continuing to knock. A distinct hollow sound could be heard. Standing back, Brandon took the Silver, and making another blade, cut a hole into the panelled wall. The piece fell to the floor and Brandon kicked it to the side. Revealed behind the panel was a button with a key hole beneath it. The digits above the button read B3.

*This is the floor!*

The Silver's intensity was building.

He pushed the button—B3. The elevator buzzed, and the door opened again on the B2 floor. No descent. The button flashed. Brandon pushed the button again. Buzz. Blink. No descent.

Brandon looked up and down the panel for a means to access this floor. He looked at the key hole at the bottom of the panel. Brandon gathered some Silver, rolled it, and smoothed it into a small, flat panel. Carefully, he fed the Silver into the key hole. The Silver formed into the shape of the key and hardened. With a slight nudge, the key turned and the button stopped its blinking. With a push and a whir, the elevator began its descent. Brandon walked out the elevator door onto floor B3.

It was darker here. The air was dry and stale. Brandon walked into the hallway. There were no doors like the previous hallway. The walls were cement—grey and substantial, like sentinel guards of something precious. At the end of the hallway was a thick door, dark grey with an electronic key pad beside it. *This is the place,* the voices whispered. Brandon looked around for other types of alarm systems. There was nothing. B3 was hidden deep enough underground that there was little chance of anyone even knowing it was here.

At the vault door, Brandon used the Silver again. After slathering the control panel completely, the door's locks clicked free in numerous places. The system was dismantled. Brandon placed his hand on the door and it slid silently into the wall. Inside was black. There was an uncanny stillness about the place and he hesitated to go in. His slight hesitation sent the Silver screaming at him to obey. Something held him back. The blackness maybe? Robotically, Brandon's hands rubbed together and smeared some Silver into his eyes. His ability to see was sufficiently amplified. He stepped into the vault.

Inside, it was larger than he anticipated. He could see four aisles stacked roof high with labelled boxes. There were filing cabinets, safes, and lockboxes. Brandon stopped as his foot brushed something on the cement floor. His eyes fell and lingered on a metal drainage hole. The cover was metal, had bars like a cage, and was imbedded into the cement floor. Brandon knelt down and touched his fingers to the bars.

Immediately a flood of memories washed over him. Descending into the sewer system, getting lost, struggling in the water . . . each memory sent arrows of emotion into his conscious mind.

Brandon looked at his hands in confusion, *what am I doing in here?* He wondered. He had been driven down here by the source. He knew it. It was inside him and drove him to many things. He looked around in wonder. He was in a vault. Where? Oh yeah—a bank. I'm in an underground, bank vault.

Fear and excitement warred as possibilities unfolded in his brain. There could be gold hidden down here, or a treasure . . . a light of curiosity lit his eyes. Suddenly, his head snapped to the side and a voice broke his reverie. The voice was strong and authoritative.

*Seek and find the secured area.*

Brandon heard the command, but his curiosity was stronger. The source's voice was fading into static of his conscience.

*Treasure* . . . , Brandon thought, 'what kind of stuff do they keep down here?' he said out loud.

He read one box down the first aisle. 45541 BRENNER FAMILY He looked at another box. This one was similar. 6693 GAETZ FAMILY He pulled the metal box off the shelf and lifted the lid. Inside was a stack of stock certificates dating back to the early 1900's.

"Whoa . . ." Brandon whispered, "This must be worth a fortune." Brandon placed the box back and continued down the aisles looking at the odd box and checking inside. There were family heirlooms, necklaces, certificates and important looking documents. Nothing of interest to a teenage boy.

As his curiosity was satisfied and his visions of gold subsided, the voice of Silver became louder and stronger. Brandon looked bewildered at first and then let go of his curiosity as he submitted once again to its control.

*Seek and find the secured area.*

Brandon obeyed. He began by walking the perimeter of the vault. In the far corner, was a small door about waist height. It was made of solid, thick, grey plastic and interlaced with steel wires. It buzzed, alive with electricity.

Brandon sat down on his knees and looked steadily at the door. Running his hands through his hair, Brandon gathered Silver, smeared it all over his hands and placed them up against wires crisscrossing the door. Electricity crackled and sent out blue sparks as Brandon easily short-circuited the system. When he removed his hands, the remaining Silver steamed. Checking himself, he found that his hands were warm, but unhurt.

Now that the electrical currents were nullified, Brandon braced his hands on the floor behind him, placed both feet on the door and pushed. The small, but heavy door,—eased open. Brandon, moved forward onto his hands and knees and crawled into the space beyond.

The door opened into a small space with a low ceiling. The space was bare except for an object in the middle of the floor. The object was a cage. It was made of a thick, slightly translucent plastic, laced with electrical wires.

A weak, red, glow emanated from the box casting a reddish tinge on the floor around the box.

*Open the cage.*

The voice inside his head pounded with anticipation. Brandon's body jolted with the force and jerked to the ground. He reached forward to touch the box.

*Open . . . the . . . cage.*

Brandon pulled the cage towards himself as he sat crunched on the floor in the small space. Rubbing his hands together, he made the Silver into a knife and proceeded to cut the top off the cage. The Silver knife began to shiver and shake. Twice, Brandon had to reshape the tool to keep it under control. His body was practically shaking and shimmering as every particle of Silver danced and waited.

Brandon finished his cut. Peering through Silver-coated eyes, he looked into the box. A cry ripped through his brain and smashed his body to the ground.

Brandon's head hit the cement and blackness seeped over him.

*       *       *

David Hensley called to the waitress. He slapped his hand on his table.

"Bring me another one of these!" He pointed to the empty mug. Rachel, who'd been waitressing at the Arlington for five years, knew what was coming.

"David," she said kindly, "You know that I always need the cash up front. No running tabs on my shift."

David reached behind him and pulled out a weathered wallet. Waving it in the air he laughed, "My dear, I will have the money for you in seconds. Just have that beer waiting for me." David stood up, teetered slightly, steadied himself and smiled. He gave Rachel an awkward nod and walked towards the door.

"Be careful you," Rachel called after him.

David Hensely adjusted his beige jacket around his small frame. "It's Red Deer, Rachel! I'll be fine!" He stepped outside and breathed in the cool night air.

Once outside, David staggered down the block to the nearby bank to access more cash from their machine. Fumbling, he opened the bank door with his bankcard and stared blankly at the hole and the glass shattered on the bank floor. He stepped around the broken glass and placed his card into the bank machine. Shaking his head of the brain fog, he entered his PIN and waited. He looked up into the mirror and rubbed his hand over the stubble that gathered in patches on his chin. A silver reflection caught his eye. Turning around, his eyes widened and he opened his mouth to scream. He lifted his hands to his face in defence. The sound of his scream fell on a silent, dark night.

# Chapter Fifteen

Tuesday, July 8<sup>th</sup>
Around 4 am

Brandon stood in an alley downtown. At this time of night, the bars were closed, the patrons long-since taxied home, and the homeless had finally found their place to rest. Even stray cats were sleeping curled up in corners amidst paper cups and newspaper inserts.

Brandon glowed silver. His arms were outspread making a T-shape. His eyes were closed. A red whip made of another gelatinous, fluid substance twisted itself around Brandon's body. The red substance wove in and out of the silver. They *pulsated* in unison. They danced. After years of separation, their beings meshed, and glowed and sparkled and swam and danced.

Using Brandon's thoughts, the Red communicated.

*I'm finally free from the cage. I knew you would find me.*

The source answered quietly, *I could always feel your presence. I knew I would find you too.*

The Red wrapped itself tighter around Brandon's body, ***I'm hungry.***

The source sent a series of commands to Brandon. *So am I.*

The Silver fairly giggled with glee as the Red wrapped itself around a stray cat and ended its life. The red whip sliced into the cat, spilling its blood and staining the pavement. Brandon stood there vacant.

Giving a measure of control over to the Red, the Silver waited as Red used Brandon to smash windows, break walls, and destroy plants. Red, in a continual winding and unwinding swirled in spirals around the boy's body, violently seeking things to destroy. Brandon robotically yielded to the commands as Red, after years of imprisonment, wreaked havoc on the downtown core.

# Chapter Sixteen

*Red Deer Advocate: Front Page*                    Date: Wednesday July 9th

Downtown Declared Unsafe

"It's confounding and upsetting that we have to warn our citizens to tread downtown with caution," stated Mayor Horst Newhanger to the press yesterday afternoon. The city is committing all resources available to stop the crimes and incarcerate the offender. In the last month, banks have been broken into, vaults opened with seemingly little effort, one man choked to death with a silver handprint, a cat was found strangled behind the 5010 Building, and windows of various shops were smashed. Officials have placed the City into emergency mode calling on all citizens to pass on any information that may lead to the capture of the culprits.

"We've faced all kinds of criminals before. This is just another reason why we need more resources poured into law enforcement." City Police Chief, Cnst. Rock change name Ruther stated, "Rest assured that we are doing everything in our power to make downtown Red Deer safe again. We will need the help of every citizen to stop the violence. This will be a community effort and good will prevail."

As most incidents of violence have occurred in the late hours downtown, police urge citizens not to venture downtown at night or alone. Any information should be directed immediately to the police at 343-0021.

When asked if anything was stolen from the vaults, the Mayor and the police were unable to release that information due to the sensitivity of the investigation.

\*   \*   \*

Dolan sat with Brooks, feet dangling off the side of the old train trestle. Both leaned forward, arms rested on the lower rail. Stars were just starting to dot the darkening sky. Below them, the Red Deer River continued its winding path through the city.

"Where do you think he took off too?"

"Beats me," answered Brooks shrugging, "His mom called for him at my house too. I haven't seen one bit of him."

"I wonder what happened to him after we split in the tunnels?"

Brooks took his time answering, "I don't know. Obviously he got out somehow—maybe he's just super ticked off at us and feels like we ditched him hardcore or something?"

Dolan shrugged, "Yeah maybe. The police are looking for him—heh, maybe we'll see his ugly mug on a milk jug?"

Silence.

"How long has he been missing now?"

"About a week or more I think," Brooks answered. He pulled out a cigarette, lit it, inhaled and passed it to Dolan. Dolan inhaled, stuck out his tongue, tried to blow a smoke ring as he exhaled, and then blew the rest out. The smoke lingered as if it wanted to hear the rest of the conversation and then dispersed with the wind.

"That is a long time to be ditching . . . do you think that he's . . . ?"

"No, I hope not."

"Yeah, I hope not too," Dolan inhaled again.

"Nervous about being here?" Dolan tuned his brown eyes onto the Brooks.

"As if. Why?"

"The great silver phantom, bonehead. It may skin you alive, suck your blood, or even strangle you to death. We are downtown you know."

Laughing, somewhat nervously, neither of them saw the glowing figure turn and step onto the far end of the bridge.

*　　*　　*

Having skipped school again, Keenan and Carlee spent their afternoon and evening sauntering around downtown selling their cigarettes. Brick buildings lined both sides of the street they walked on. It was dusk and stars were beginning to awaken as the sun slowly lost its strength. The business community was long gone, and even the last patrons of the soup kitchen had exited with full bellies.

"I wish we could've gone for dinner in there. I'm starved."

"Me too," Carlee replied, "But you know the rules—if we're caught at a soup kitchen they'll take us away from Mom."

"Maybe that isn't so bad."

Carlee looked at Keenan and looked away, "Maybe it isn't so good."

With that, they both stood up. They began the long walk home to Highland Green via the old train bridge.

# Chapter Seventeen

Wednesday, July 9<sup>th</sup>
Dusk

The boy who was once Brandon, stood at the end of the bridge. He stared at the kids laughing and hanging over the railing. Swirling colours of silver swam around his body. Interlaced with the Silver was the thick Red vein that coursed in congruent spirals around his body slicing in and out of him like a serpent and constantly moving. Rage and passion both bridled inside of him.

Brandon watched.

Suddenly, a vague sense of familiarity began to creep its way into Brandon's brain. He somehow knew the two people at the end of the bridge. This thought began to widen a gap. A gap between his own real thoughts and the Silver controlled ones. A longing for . . . something . . . began to grow and this turned down the volume on the Silver's voices. It was like listening to a stereo, and then turning it down so you can hear your own thoughts. Loneliness. It began to knock as timidly as a mouse on the cage that imprisoned his mind, begging to be heard, felt and acknowledged. The source was losing control.

*Stop his emotions!* Screamed the Red through violent impulses. *You have to keep control!*

The Silver scattered signals, voices, and suggestions in a random frenzy.

The Red vein curled in tighter and lashed in and around Brandon's body like a whip, inflicting lacerations. The wounds only drove larger wedges into the gap as jolts of pain stimulated his mind.

The word 'friend' formed itself on Brandon's frontal lobe. Fireworks blasted into his conscience. The Red began to grow limp and sagged off his body. The mere suggestion of the word 'friend' was wrought with memories of kickball, lighting fires with hairspray, crawling into a manhole . . . with this last memory a tidal wave hit his brain and the powerful Silver hostage buckled to his knees.

Brandon held his hands to his head as the war for control of his mind raged like a mad bull, trapped in a ring trying to get rid of the matador.

In the silence following their laughter, Dolan and Brooks looked out at the distorted reflections of the stars reflected in the river below. A bright reflection off the water caused both of them to look up to the end of the bridge. Their arms went rigid as they saw the glowing figure.

"It's the phantom" gasped Brooks.

"Y-e-a-h . . ." Dolan couldn't tear his eyes away.

As they watched, the phantom crumpled to the ground, shattering silver light everywhere. Brooks and Dolan stood frozen. They looked at each other nervously.

"Is he hurt or something?" Dolan asked, "Look at him."

Brooks looked again trying to see what Dolan was talking about. He then realized the phantom was rocking back and forth cradling his head.

"Or is he preparing to attack?"

"We need to go. Now." Brooks was insistent. He grabbed Dolan's arm, stood up, and began dragging him back towards the bike trails.

"No," Dolan shook his arm loose and stopped. He hadn't taken his eyes off the phantom yet.

"Look at him Brooks. He's glowing . . . silver." Brooks let go of Dolan's shirt and turned towards the phantom.

"Silver," Dolan repeated the word slowly, "There was that goop in the tunnels . . ."

Brooks paused . . . "You don't think . . . do you?"

Dolan nodded. "It has to be. What else would it be?" Dolan began to walk forward towards the phantom.

"Stop Dolan!" Brooks whispered loudly, "He'll kill you!"

Dolan was mesmerized and continued to walk forward. "Please," Brooks whispered and stepped in front of him. He had to walk backwards now because Dolan wasn't stopping.

"I just have to see . . ." Dolan left the sentence hanging.

\*     \*     \*

Keenan and Carlee crouched on a small rise watching the phantom as it crumpled to the ground.

"We need to get away Keenan!" Carlee whispered frantically.

The rise they were laying behind was far enough away that they were well hidden in the shadows of the night.

"I want to see more," whispered Keenan.

Carlee opened her mouth to respond, but thought silence was more prudent considering the potential danger. They stared as two figures on the bridge began to walk towards the phantom.

\*     \*     \*

"Brandon?"

The voice was familiar. The name was familiar. Still holding his head, Brandon lifted his eyes up to the voice. But, there was no recognition.

"Brandon."

The voice was firmer this time. Aggressive? He slowly rose to his feet, fingers melding and working the silver fire. His glowing, blank eyes stared at the two figures in front of him. The two figures were fifteen feet away. They were standing there. They were looking at him.

Confronting. Him.


Dolan looked at Brandon at bit nervously now. Something, in the space of a second—changed.

"Brandon, it's me—Dolan. This is Brooks. Remember? We've been looking all over for you."

No response.

"Your mom's worried sick." "Brandon . . . uh . . ." Dolan stumbled for words, "See my foot, I broke my ankle in the tunnel." He lifted up his half cast to show Brandon.

Brooks jumped in, "Remember the tunnels? Dolan, you . . . me, getting lost . . . we couldn't find you . . . but here you are now. Here we are . . ." his words dribbled off as he realized they were having no effect.


Inside Brandon was a furnace of energy preparing to explode. Inside, the source was reorganizing its offence. It began sending out waves of euphoria to distract Brandon from his emotions. This host would remain controlled. The Silver whispered, soothed, caressed and called his name.

Red was furious. ***Take him by force. Give me control of this host. I'll strangle him like the cat.***

The Silver source ignored the Red's rant and continued with the task at hand.

Brandon continued to stand still. The Silver could do nothing without its host's consent.

The Red was violent, whipping and lashing one second, limp and sagging the next. It waited for the Silver to gain control.

The silence in that moment was thick. If the silence came from Dairy Queen, you could turn it upside down and the spoon wouldn't fall out.

Still, Brandon did not move.

Dolan and Brooks began to shuffle.

Dolan ventured out, "Can we take you home Brandon?"

At the word 'home' a tear forced its way from Brandon's eye and ran down his cheek. Where the tear touched Silver, steam lifted into the air. Rivulets of Silver slithered out of the way. A small, imperceptible scream echoed as molecules of Silver dissolved in the path of that one lone tear.

"That's Dolan and Brooks," Keenan whispered excitedly, "They're talking with the phantom.

"It doesn't look like the phantom is talking back," Carlee responded quietly.

Keenan rose up from his stomach and immediately Carlee pounced on him. Whispering forcefully for him to stay down, Keenan sunk back to his stomach. They crouched behind the rise, hidden in the shadows, and watched.

The moment was intense. Dolan and Brooks looked at each other not knowing what to do. Brandon stood stalk-still. His eyes were a maze of confusion. Unreadable. Once, his eyes seemed to lighten with recognition, but then quickly they'd glaze back into blankness. Recognition, then blankness. The moment lingered uncomfortably.

Dolan scuffed some tar with the toe of his foot, shifted his weight off onto his casted foot, and opened his mouth to speak again when he froze. Brandon was moving. His eyes were swimming with the Silver, focusing and refocusing. His glowing lips parted and with great effort, Brandon forced out one word to Brooks and Dolan.

"Run."

It looked as though Brandon were about to explode. Flashings of Silver and whips of Red lightening began to vibrate and cripple the air around him.

"But Brandon . . ." Dolan started but quickly stopped as the liquid Silver began to form and deform in Brandon's hand.

They ran. They ran hard. They ran without looking back. Dolan's cast made a loud thumping sound as he fought to keep up with Brooks.

At the end of the bridge, they ducked underneath and ran to the water's edge—hiding in the shadows of the bridge's cement pillars below. Gasping and clutching their sides, they each peered out from behind the pillar in time to watch the explosion.

Seeing Dolan and Brooks run for their lives, Keenan threw his arm around Carlee and pulled her down to the grass. They pressed themselves into the ground seconds before blades of Silver sliced the air where they just were.

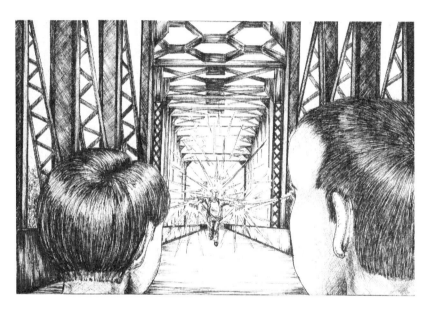

*It looked as though Brandon were about to explode.*

# Chapter Eighteen

Seeing Dolan and Brooks take off running, Brandon held onto his conscious for as long as he could. It was two wills against one. In the end, his was weaker. Control for his mind, and thereby his body, tore apart his defences. Piece by piece, his mind was being over taken. Piece by piece, he was broken down until his will-power was depleted. Unable to continue, he dropped all of his defences. Out of what seemed to be pure vengeance, the Silver erupted.

The Silver boiled beneath his skin, and then shot out in pinpointed blades through his pores. His skin shred and split, exposing the muscle beneath. Blood began to drip and puddle, staining the wood where he stood. The blades of Silver sliced through the air, sizzling, cracking, and embedding themselves into the wood of the bridge and slicing anything that was in its way. After the eruption, there was silence. The river swallowed the Silver blades as they sliced over the bridge rails to fall into the water below.

Brandon's body collapsed to the ground. The fight was over. His blood, his life fluid, intoxicated with the Silver, sparkled and twinkled like falling stars as it dripped through the old ties and into the river below.

Brandon's face lay against the trestle's wood. His eyes were empty. His mind, now a vacuum, was filled only with Silver's impulses. Slowly, Silver began to slide out of his mouth and to swarm and coat his body like a blanket.

Brandon's lungs breathed.

The Red, still wrapped around his body, vibrated and glowed, but stayed silent. It had forgotten how powerful the Silver could be.

The whispers returned. He felt their cool, comforting presence as they brought relief to his burning body, and healing to his shredded skin. Moments passed. A cool wind blew through the river valley and lifted the hairs on his head. Breathing deeply, Brandon pulled himself up off the rough wooden tiers on the old train bridge and stood. He looked around. The Silver had sliced through parts of the bridge leaving chunks of wood scattered around. Puddles of Silver lay where they had stabbed and scarred the wood. No longer blades, but puddles.

The puddles began to move inch by inch. They crawled and dropped between the ties and into the river below. Turning, he walked woodenly off the trestle bridge, and back towards downtown.

Keenan and Carlee lay still as the glowing phantom walked past them. They could see his clothing ripped, torn, and plastered to his skin with wet blood. He looked horrifying. A Red whip circled him and spiralled around his body. He walked woodenly and forcefully, alive and sparkling.

Their bodies pressed to the ground, they barely lifted their heads to get a better look. As the glowing phantom turned a corner downtown, Keenan and Carlee lifted themselves off the ground. They began to shiver.

"That was unbelievable. We've seen the phantom. What do we do now Carlee?"

Carlee looked at Keenan and rubbed her bare arms. Goose bumps were covering them.

"Keenan, didn't you recognize the phantom?"

"What are you talking about?"

"It's Brandon. That was Brandon. He almost killed them. Almost killed us."

Keenan looked in the direction Brandon had taken. He took a step forward to follow, "You're sure?"

"Positive. Why do you think Dolan and Brooks were talking with him?"

Keenan nodded.

"We could've been killed. That was close," Carlee said, as Keenan continued to look in the direction of Brandon.

"Let's go home and see what Dolan and Brooks want to do. If we move fast, we can beat them there."

Keenan nodded again. He glanced one more time towards downtown, and they both took off at a slow jog.


Brooks and Dolan sat under the bridge catching their breath. Neither of them said anything. They just stared at the placid river water. Finally, their breathing slowed and their panic abated—they looked at each other.

"Is it safe?" Brooks asked seriously.

"Oh yeah," Dolan said with a hint of a grin, "That was insane!"

"Can you believe that was Brandon?" "Is he dead or alive? Or just half alive?" He would've killed us . . ." Brooks last comment hung on the air like laundry.

Dolan's grin disintegrated. "It's possible," Dolan started slowly, "It seemed like he was out of control or something. Maybe that silver stuff from the sewers is controlling him and it was what wanted to kill us."

"But why?"

"Yet," Dolan continued his train of thought, "Yet he still had control enough to tell us to run . . . but then he lost control . . ."

"He is outta control, I think." Brooks stood and began walking back up the incline to the top of the bridge. "Should we go to the police?"

"Yeah, I guess—but they might just shoot him—what if there is still hope for him?"

"Hope for what?" Brooks was standing on the bridge looking out over the water again.

"Hope for Brandon."

Dolan hobbled up, joined Brooks and both of them walked across the bridge to where Brandon was last seen. They walked carefully and avoided pulsating Silver puddles as they crossed the bridge.

"Do you really think there is hope for Brandon—or will we have to go to the police so they can . . . uh . . . deal with him?"

Dolan knelt down and stared at a circular glob of Silver. Its glow cast a light over his face.

"You know, this stuff saved my life in the sewers, yet it is taking Brandon's life . . . sucking away the real Brandon . . . what in the world is this crap?"

Brooks squatted now too, "Don't get so close man, it's way more dangerous than we thought. I bettcha' it's toxic."

Dolan looked around, grabbed a twig from off the bridge ties, and dipped it into the puddle. It glowed slightly stronger and began to climb the twig up to Dolan's fingers. Quickly, Dolan shook the Silver off and threw the twig over the side rail.

Brooks, stared in wonder.


"It's almost like a web—it doesn't harm you until you're stuck in it and then you can't get out,"

Brooks looked at Dolan, "And every web has a spider."

Dolan replied, a gleam in his eye, "Every spider also has an enemy."

# Chapter Nineteen

July 10<sup>th</sup>
City Hall

The room was quiet and still as officials read the report on the table in front of them. His Worship, Mayor Horst Newhanger was there, along with the Chief of police, the City Bank district president, and a couple military soldiers in camouflage. Standing at the front of the room was Corporal James Richard in full army gear, feet spread and arms crossed. He chewed on his upper lip, stared at the group in the room, and waited impatiently for them to finish reading.

Mayor Horst Newhanger was the first to look up from the report. His cowboy hat was sitting on the table in front of him like a favourite pet. He took his glasses off and placed them meticulously beside his notepad. He brought his thumb and forefinger to his nose and rubbed the bridge vigorously before putting his glasses back on. This was his fourth year as Mayor of Red Deer and he was planning on running again in the coming fall election. The past election had been close and he had won because of the strong religious vote in the city. This next election, he might not be so lucky. It was important that this entire situation be used to elevate his position in the eyes of the citizens and not leave him looking like the blundering idiot he was feeling like. *Pull yourself together Horst, you can handle this guy.* He looked up at the Corporal, usurping his authority at the table, and straightened his resolve. This Corporal James was stealing his thunder.

He glanced again at the gun strapped across the corporal's chest, "This is . . . insane," he stated slapping the report on the table, "You're telling me there is more than just this silver . . . stuff?"

Corporal James just stared at Horst and turned his eyes to the others in the room indicating their chance to give a response.

"How long has this," Chief Rock Ruther looked at the report again, "This Silver . . . this Silver life form been hidden in our city?"

Corporal James puckered his lips and breathed out slowly. "Actually, the Silver Toxinate, as it is called, has never been in our custody. We were unable to . . . control its influence on some of our officers. It got away, so to speak. Up until recently, we haven't had any reports of the Toxinate showing up anywhere. The last known report, though it was fairly vague, was from a small village on the east coast of Mexico reporting a silver chemical in the water. Officials were delayed in assessing the situation due to a hurricane that blew in right around that time. Since then, the Silver Toxinate has been quiet.

It was the Red Toxinate that was in custody in an electrically magnetized, airtight cage, in an electrically controlled vault, deep underground. It is this Red Toxinate that has been released, presumably by a victim under the control of the Silver Toxinate or so it would seem."

Mayor Newhanger again put up his hand, somehow feeling like a schoolboy in this Corporal's presence. "So we have seen the damage the Silver stuff can do, but what about the Red? Is it worse or the same? Can we capture these Toxinates? How did they come to be? . . ."

Corporal James put up his hand, palm forward as a gesture to stop.

"As you know, there was another attack downtown last night on the Fairview bridge. Much of the information we know about the Silver and the Red Toxinate comes only from the damage that ensues. The damage seems to be concentrated in the downtown area, and with each incident we are gaining a little more knowledge. From the small amounts of Toxinate left at the scenes, our scientists are working in a high security, highly supervised lab trying to dissect its properties. We know that both Toxinates are liquid or gelatine in form, but work in separate ways.

The Silver, if taken in, works like a drug.

The Red, a violent mixture of toxinates, works by force. Both work using the mind of a human. They need a host. Without a host, they are in a sense, sterile. Toxic, but harmless.

The Silver Toxinate seems to be self-perpetuating. There is a never-ending supply coming from the source.

The Red Toxinate is what it is, and by itself does not reproduce.

"Where did they come from?" Mayor Newhanger interrupted.

Corporal James continued without missing a beat. "The history of these Toxinates is sketchy at best. Our experts tell us they were brought back from an excavation of rock in the US Mars expeditions. We have reports of scientists performing feats of great strength, and many falling prey to its control and losing their minds. Most of these reports were burnt or hidden, and we have built our case on rumours and leaked information. How the Silver Toxinate got here to Red Deer, Alberta remains a mystery.

The Silver Toxinate seems to thrive in water and is able to travel great distances once in a water system. It is entirely possible that it somehow floated here or latched itself onto fish or boats to come this far north. That is speculation of course."

"Tell me please, why would you hide or secure this Red Toxinate in our city, in the basement of a bank? And why not on your military base?" The Mayor crossed his arms and sunk bank into his chair.

Mr. Farley, the bank president opened his mouth to speak and with a look from the Corporal, shut it. "There were some worries among the higher officials that there would be some tampering with the Red Toxinate in an attempt to use it as a weapon," stated the Corporal turning his attention back to the Mayor. "The Red Toxinate, once captured, was secretly lifted away from the base and hidden here in Red Deer."

"And why Red Deer?" The Mayor's eyes were growing wider.

"Red Deer is just one of those cities. It's a place that's average. There's not too much violence. There's not too many people. People were living in Red Deer because they didn't want big city jobs and big city power. On top of that, no one would ever look in a bank vault. The City Bank, being one of the oldest in the city, was built with the vault deep in the ground. We had a space specially constructed within the vault to imprison the Red Toxinate."

"How long ago was this?"

"Forty three years ago."

"Can they be captured?"

At this point, the Corporal looked sternly at the Mayor and spoke quietly, "We will capture them Mr. Newhanger. Don't underestimate our ability. You will cooperate with us."

This was more of a statement and not a question. Mayor Horst gave a curt nod in return.

"We will need passes and unsupervised access to every government-owned building to begin with." Mayor Horst opened his mouth to protest, his glasses falling down to the end of his bulbous nose, "But we have . . . ," his voice faltered at the look from Corporal James.

The Corporal looked at the Bank Administrator.

"You have our complete cooperation," Mr. Carl Farely answered, pushing his glasses up to the bridge of his nose.

"Right." A quick look and nod between the Chief of Police and the Corporal.

"This meeting is adjourned. Ruther, meet me at the station in forty-five minutes for a full scale debrief."

Mr. Farely, Mayor Newhanger and Chief Rock Ruther all stood up to leave. No one was saying much.

"And one more thing," his voice sounded unnervingly loud in the quiet space, "This is highly classified information. If any of this leaks, I'll know who to come and arrest."

With that, Corporal James turned on the heel of his black boot and with a stomp left the room.

# Chapter Twenty

July 24<sup>th</sup>
Morning

"Where are you going Dolan?" Carlee asked innocently, "Why are you dressed like that?"

A couple weeks had passed since the incident on the bridge. Keenan and Carlee had kept quiet hoping that Dolan would be the one to bring it up. He didn't. As far as they knew, Dolan hadn't called the cops, so they didn't either. Dolan had been irritable at home, frustrating to be around and overly eager to be rid of the half cast that limited all his activities. Finally, the doctor had agreed and the cast was removed. That was this morning.

Dolan glanced over his shoulder at Carlee as he slipped on his rubber boots. A black toque was pulled down low over his ears, and he had a backpack hanging low over his baggy skater jeans. He paused and then turned to face her directly.

"Mind your business. It's style you don't even know about." Dolan shrugged into his backpack and walked out the door.

Staring after him through the broken screen, Carlee motioned to Keenan.

"What's our brother up to?" Keenan asked.

"Something . . . something . . . we need to find out about," Carlee answered, still watching as Dolan disappeared down the street. "Come on, let's follow him!"

Carlee grabbed Keenan's hand and dragged him out the door. Keenan hesitated.

"Come on, or we'll lose him."

"Something feels . . . wrong about this, sis."

Carlee looked into Keenan's eyes for what would be the last time in long time, "We're doing this for Dolan, Keenan. He needs us."

Keenan shrugged and followed.

Carlee would look back on this day and wish she had stayed inside and watched television.

They kept to the edges of the houses and bushes and trees, a fair distance back, but close enough that they kept Dolan in their sights.

At first, it was easy to follow him. He met up with Brooks at the North Hill Store. Brooks was dressed the same all in black with rubber boots as well. Together they continued walking. They went down the hill towards the river. Once they reached the trails, Dolan and Brooks continued on following the path for a short distance. Keenan and Carlee followed on the bike trails keeping one bend behind them so they wouldn't be seen.

"Where are they going?" Carlee wondered aloud as they continued to sneak down the path.

The game of hide and follow continued for a ways down the bike paths by the river, when suddenly, Brooks and Dolan stopped. They veered off to the left side of the path into the trees and shrubs lining the riverbank. Keenan and Carlee also slipped into the brush after them and quietly knelt down to watch.

Dolan took off his backpack and pulled out an old crowbar. He wedged it into the grates and began to heave on the end. Brooks ran over to help.

Together, they pried the crusted grate off the hole. Heaving, both of them pushed it to the side.

"Man, this lid hasn't been moved in years!" Brooks exclaimed.

"All the better for us. Means there are less people that know about it."

"You go first. Good thing you had that stink'n cast taken off this morning."

"Yeah, it did stink." Dolan stretched his leg and ankle and then slipped over the edge into the darkness of the tunnels.

"I totally remember this," Dolan stated as they began to work through the sludge. He paused to look back through the hole and up into the sunlight outside.

"Why are we choosing this hole to start off?" Brooks asked as he dropped down beside him.

It was musty, dark and dank. Already, Brooks was grateful that they had brought rubber boots.

"What are we going to do if the water levels rise again?"

Dolan opened up his backpack and showed Brooks the rope, flashlights and other items he had thought to bring.

"I can't believe I am back in here so soon . . . I didn't think I'd ever come back."

"Me neither," Dolan replied.

They both paused and looked into the darkness around them. There it was. Silver glowed softly in patches on the tunnel walls.

"I chose this spot, because I'm pretty sure this is sorta close to where we lost Brandon . . . of course, I could be totally off. I think the tunnels took us this way before dumping me in the river. If the water rises again, we'll find a manhole. That's what the rope is for . . . if one of us gets up on the ladder, the other can lower the rope. We have to make sure we don't lose each other again."

Dolan handed Brooks a flashlight. They each swung their beams around. Fixing left, Dolan started forward.

"We should make sure we try not to touch the silver at all, eh? The stuff is obviously not what it seems."

Brooks needed no encouragement to refrain. Together they moved along in silence.

The tunnel, though somewhat refreshing with its coolness, would soon become a landmine of devastation.


Keenan and Carlee watched as they disappeared into the sewer. They waited in silence. Looking at each other, Keenan nodded at Carlee, Carlee gave a slight nod in return. Getting up, they both made their way to the sewer hole.

The drop from bright sunlight into black darkness left their pupils fighting to adjust. Both stood a second before moving. Carlee looked down at the sunlight puddling around her feet. She breathed in the dank air. "Keenan?" she whispered.

Keenan had his hands in his hair and was looking down the tunnel, "Yeah?"

"You ready for this?"

"Yeah," Keenan answered. He stepped into the darkness.


"What exactly are we looking for?" Brooks asked, breaking their silent reverie.

They had been walking slowly for about ten minutes. Each of them caught up in his own thoughts and memories. Dolan took his time in answering. Stopping, Dolan shone the light up against the wall.

"Watch," he instructed. He held his light up, shining along the wall.

"Watch the Silver closely."

With that said, he inched forward, all the while holding the light so it shone on the concrete. At first, nothing happened, but as the light passed over the Silver and left it in the shadows, it began to move along the wall towards Dolan. Dolan stopped moving. The Silver continued to slither until it stopped just outside of the light of the flashlight. He looked up at Brooks.

"Uh, this doesn't answer my question," Brooks stated in confusion.

"Actually it does," Dolan explained as he moved the light again onto the Silver.

Brooks watched again as the Silver began to move away out of the light and into the shadows. Dolan again began to move forward, and again the Silver slithered after him. Dolan stopped and looked at Brooks.

"The Silver knows we're here. It's following us."

# Chapter Twenty One

Somewhere Deep below the city

Brandon lay face down on the ground in the tunnel. Silver swarmed all over him, like ants restless after having their nest disturbed. He didn't move. He didn't speak. He didn't think. His body lay awaiting its next command.

The source, the 'heart and brain' of the Silver, continued to pulse a steady rhythm inside his body, continually reproducing and pumping Silver into and through Brandon's veins. Glowing fluid pulsed inside of him making his translucent skin glow. The mercury-like substance glittered outside of him; liquid and constantly changing shape. A disturbance rippled slightly through the core causing the Silver to light up momentarily. A command was impulsed and released. In this way, the source was able to communicate with its widespread 'body.' Within a certain distance it could send out an electronic impulse. The impulse would light up the Silver momentarily before it was released to the next nearest Silver patch. The impulses carried messages delivered to and from the source.

All along the tunnels, the Silver began to twinkle as the next command was issued.

Brandon lay still. He felt the command more than he heard it. He stirred. Slowly, his body responded. He turned onto his belly and began to crawl back out into the tunnels.

*     *     *

Keenan and Carlee were ill prepared to be in the sewer tunnels. Their shoes became heavy with sludge and threatened to slip off into the mud with every step. They tried to breathe warmth onto their cold hands. Following Dolan and Brooks wasn't difficult as the pair had left streaks on the wall where their hands had touched the walls.

"What is this glowing stuff on the walls?" Carlee asked.

"Not sure," answered Keenan, "It gives us a bit of light though, eh?"

"Yeah, that's good." Carlee reached up with a curious hand to touch the silver ooze.

Instantly it grew brighter, calling her to touch. Keenan watched, fascinated. Feeling compelled, he reached towards the same splatter that Carlee was reaching. It glowed brighter. He pulled away and it dulled.

"Should we be touching it?" Carlee asked tentatively.

Keenan's eyes glowed Silver with the reflection, "I want to . . ." Keenan reached forward. The glow in his eyes was no longer a reflection, but a pool. There was an intensity coming from inside him "I . . . really . . . want . . . to." Keenan whispered again.

"Keenan, stop." Keenan was entranced. "Keenan STOP!"

Carlee grabbed Keenan's hand and threw it down. Immediately, anger rose up like snake in Keenan, his eyes lit up and he roared at Carlee, "Don't touch me!"

Carlee looked from his eyes, down to the hand now grabbing her wrist, and back up again. Keenan was back, angry, but back.

"Keenan, give your head a shake. You don't have to get all ticked off. The stuff was affecting you."

"You've got no clue what you're talking about."

Keenan turned abruptly and continued to walk through the tunnels.

"I saw you Keenan," Carlee called after him. She had seen what the silver goup had done to him.

Carlee ran up behind him, "Keenan?"

"Shut up."

Keenan cut her off short without looking at her, "You don't know what you are talking about."

"But I . . ."

"SHUT UP!"

His voice echoed and silenced. Carlee dropped her gaze to her feet.

Truth was the Silver was calling to him. He felt it. And not just from the spot on the wall. It was calling from inside him. It felt good. It felt strong. He felt a need for it.

*How is this possible? Is it calling me or am I just craving it?*

He stole a glance at Carlee as she walked beside him.

*If only she hadn't pulled his arm away . . . . Why did the desire fade so quickly . . .* these thoughts continued as they made their way through the tunnels.

Glancing again at Carlee, he slowed his pace so they were walking side by side. Keeping his right hand in his pocket and letting his left hand drift, he let it swing naturally by his side. When he spotted the silver at waist height, he let his hand swing up against the wall. Carlee didn't notice a thing as he slid his glowing hand back into his pocket.

*   *   *

Brooks and Dolan continued following the Silver path. It was easy to do, as it seemed to shine brighter now than it had before. The deeper they penetrated, the more Silver there was. There were continual off shoots that glowed bleakly and others that had no Silver at all. They simply followed the path that was lit up the most.

"I think something is a bit different," remarked Brooks, "It is like I can sense a change or something."

"Me too . . . something . . ." Dolan stopped and looked around. "Something . . ."

Brooks watched as Dolan stepped up to the wall. The Silver all around him immediately grew brighter.

"It's like it's been charged with an electric current or something," Brooks stated, "Are we safe?"

"Yes. I think so. As long as we don't touch it—we're safe. It can't jump off the wall at us—or it would've already. It needs our contact— our permission, so to speak."

"So what are we going to do if Brandon tries to kill us again? You know this might happen, especially if it knows we are here."

"Yeah . . . I'm not sure—all I know is that whatever happens we cannot let the Silver touch us or more importantly get inside us."

"Brandon did warn us though."

"Yeah. He did. He knew us, but it took a lot out of him to do so."

Brooks leaned over, rested his hands on his knees and looked ahead, "So . . . the key then, is getting him to know who we are . . . ?"

Dolan looked at Brooks and smiled. "You've hit the monkey with the hammer. We have to bombard Brandon with memories of us. We have to remind him of home. We have to draw him out like . . . like reeling a fish out of the river."

They both looked ahead, a bit more confident than before and continued on.

They were so lost in their thoughts they didn't notice that they had begun to duck their heads a bit as the tunnels were coming smaller. Around them, clusters of Silver continued to glow and grow into larger and larger patches.

\*     \*     \*

Following the trail marks of the boys in front them, Keenan and Carlee continued forward. Keenan, hand in his pocket, began to finger the coolness of the Silver. He let it crawl up his hand and wrist and slip between his fingers. It was enticing to have it crawl up his arm and slide back down into his pocket again. It sang to him. Called to him. He could hear it loudly, and wondered if Carlee could hear it too.

He felt a strong urge to become one with this substance. He pulled his hand out of his pocket. The song lessened in strength, but the call was there. It was in his head. He put his hand back in and the song brought a smile to his lips.

Keenan, glanced at Carlee again and slowed his pace slightly so that he could be behind her, out of sight. Keenan pulled out the Silver and stared at it. A thousand flecks swirled in the jelly he held in the palm of his hand. The voices became stronger. His face reflected its glow in the darkness. Hesitantly, he brought the Silver to his eyes. The flecks swarmed, danced and pulsed pulling him into their colours. His body painfully throbbing, Keenan, eyes wide, brought the Silver and rubbed it into his eyes.

Immediately, the light was blinding and the coolness saturated all of his senses. He stood blinking as each fleck of Silver swam into the warm flesh of their new host. An assault of pleasure, extreme pleasure, took over his body as he stood and bathed in its invasion. Carlee, aware that something was amiss, turned and saw Keenan standing there. His face shone, his head was back and his glow was Silver.

Carlee stopped, and stared. His face glowed like a ghost. Like Brandon.

Confused thoughts raced through Carlee's head as she looked at Keenan in shock.

*What was he doing? He took in the silver stuff somehow . . . what had he done? . . . What was he thinking? Was he like Brandon now? Will he try and kill me? I have to warn Dolan and Brooks . . . why?*

"Keenan," she started back towards him and stopped.

Keenan had his head tilted back and Silver steaming down from his eyes like toxic tears, turned and faced Carlee. "Leave me!" His voice was rough and loud.

Her insides began to tighten. Keenan never yelled like that.

"Leave me, now!" Keenan raised his arms threateningly.

Carlee turned and ran.

She couldn't shake the image. It was almost as if he was being taken over by something. Like he was giving himself over, surrendering willingly.

*Why?*

She kept running.

The tunnels continued to get lighter as more and more Silver covered the walls like moss in a damp forest. Breathing heavier, sides aching, Carlee stopped to get her bearings. Her breath was laboured and she was sweating now. Thick dark hair fell heavily on her back and dark bangs hung in her eyes. Pulling the hair out of her face, she checked behind her.

No sign of Keenan. This was good.

However, being in these tunnels was not good. She felt an overwhelming desire to be out in the sunshine away from this artificially lit sewer. *What was she doing here? What could she do to help Brandon?* Her emotions hit her hard. She was alone. She was lost. No one knew she was down here. For all she knew, death was as near as Brandon was. And Keenan . . . she couldn't bear it. Sitting down on some hardened sludge, she pulled her legs up to her chin and began to weep.

All around her, Silver pulsed and glowed.

# Chapter Twenty Two

July 24<sup>th</sup>
Early afternoon

City Hall held little interest for Corporal James. There was nothing in the archives that he hadn't already discovered from other sources. The bank had been only somewhat useful.

Mr. Carl Farely had led him and the Chief down into the deepest basement of the bank. After ducking inside and seeing for himself that the cage was empty, he had checked the vault door for signs of entry. Sure enough, traces of Silver Toxinate were enmeshed in the circuitry of the security system.

"Mr. Farely."

The mousy banker knelt down and peeked his nose into the vault where the corporal was crouched. His glasses again falling to the end of his nose. Corporal James glanced at the nose. There was something odd about this banker and he just couldn't place it. He seemed to know very little about the Toxinate, and was just a little too eager to be compliant.

"Yes?"

The Corporal was inside the vault, laying on his stomach studying the door.

"I want this fixed immediately. Double the wiring, and triple the voltage."

He saw a hand push the glasses up to the bridge of his nose.

"Yes sir." Carl answered.

Carl waited to see if there was any other orders. Hearing none, he stood up and waited.

Chief Rock Ruther was standing to the side of the door up against the wall, his hands clasped behind his broad back stretching his uniform over his large frame.

"Is there anything else dangerous down here I should know about?" He didn't look at the banker, but let his eyes sweep around the vault.

The voice that responded was quick and sharp, "Nope. Only private documents belonging to private families."

"It must cost a lot of cash to have your stuff stored in a place like this . . . ," Ruther pulled on his left ear."

"Uh . . . yeah . . . it can add up for sure."

Ruther glanced sideways at the banker. He was rocking back and forth on the balls of his feet. *He sure seems awfully comfortable down here* he thought.

Corporal James crawled out and both men turned to wait for his report. He had studied the reports of these Intoxicates. They preferred damp areas and seemed to love the water. They weren't going to be anywhere around here. Walking back through the vault, he paused and looked at the grate on the ground where water would drain if the vault flooded. He knew exactly where he would look next. Wordlessly, Chief Ruther followed and Mr. Farely locked the door.

\*      \*      \*

Rock Ruther walked through the main doors of the water treatment plant. A security guard met them in the foyer.

"Are you sure you want to search here?" the Chief asked with a grimace on his face. "The place reeks to high heaven."

Corporal James, standing erect, was looking out over the river. He turned only his head, and gave Ruther a sneer and a nod and then turned his head forward again. Ruther opened the door wider and stepped through. The water treatment plant was made largely of cement and the building was old. You could see water stains of various colors and designs streaking the walls and floor seams.

"I want to see the treatment area, beginning with the sludge tanks," the Corporal James ordered, "Immediately."

Rising in front of them were a number of massive steel cylinders. These cylinders were eight meters across and eleven meters high. Four cubic meters of sewage, thick, and dark, sat processing in each cylinder. The smell was overpowering.

Corporal James stood and looked into the inky sewage. They weren't here. He was sure of it. Ploughing through this mess would be a last resort. "Next," he spoke again to the guard without providing eye contact. These pathetic security guards in uniform drove him crazy. They were a disgrace to the profession of public protection. In his mind, all security belonged to the army and should be under their jurisdiction.

Next, the security guard escorted Rock and James down through passageways, up a flight of stairs and onto a low catwalk that overlooked pools of water. Some of the pools were still. Others were swirling patterns of greys and dull greens.

The Corporal leaned against the metal catwalk railing and stared down. He was silent. He watched the whirlpools spin.

Chief Ruther stood back a bit to give this Corporal some room. He wasn't used to following a tyrant around like an obedient puppy dog. He sighed silently and let his mind escape to his duties after work. He mentally walked through a short list of things to do and decided to pick up a treat for his daughter Emily.

Corporal James stood up and Chief Ruther brought his mind back to the present.

"It's not here," he said finally, "We'd know it if it was. Move on."

Ruther exhaled. He hadn't realized he was holding his breath.

"Take me where the water first comes in from the river. This is where we need to look."

James' orders were getting annoying.

The lights were dimmer here below ground and the water was flowing from the river, falling over a cement wall and crashing into a large, cement, holding tank.

"That is where the water first enters the building. That water," the security guard stated pointing down into the tank, "is water right from the river. You can see that it is still translucent. There's not much debris. This is thanks to our community cleaning crew. We recently had sixty volunteers working along the river banks—"

Corporal James lifted up his hand, "I'm not a tourist."

The security guard's mouth shut and he turned away.

Chief Ruther shook his head with disgust at the Corporal's rudeness. *I'll be glad to find these Toxinates just to get rid of this butthead,* he thought to himself. Chief Rock Ruther was a kind-hearted man with a big smile for most people. Working with Corporal James and his incessant seriousness, was starting to sour his own demeanour. He felt he couldn't really be himself around this strict grump. Work should be fun. The public face of the police needed to be safe, not fearsome. Chief Ruther stretched his mouth into a tight smile and quickly got serious again as the Corporal stirred.

Corporal James turned to the police chief. He chewed on his bottom lip and breathed out through his nose. It sounded wheezy. Chief Ruther's eyes went to the Corporal's nose. Black hairs poked out from the tip.

*Disgusting* he thought, *learn to shave and pluck.*

Self-consciously he brought his own hand up under the pretence of wiping to make sure he didn't have any unrulies poking out. Chief Ruther prided himself on his clean-shaven face, and his straight teeth. He was good looking. He knew it. The public in Red Deer loved him and respected him. The wheezing continued. Distracted, the Chief tried to focus on something else. His eyes dropped down to the Corporal's uniform. He blinked. He looked discretely at it again.

Yeah, there was hair sticking out between the buttons on his uniform.

*Disgusting.*

Chief Ruther worked out every morning at the cop shop. After his shower, he proudly smoothed various creams across his broad chest and plucked any of the stray hairs that grew around his nipples. He would often spend time in the mirror admiring his smooth skin.

An awful vision of the Corporal without clothes looking as hairy as an ape walked into his imagination.

*Disgusting.*

Shaking his head to clear the horrid vision, the Chief turned back to the water.

Corporal James continued to look at the Chief, but his mind was elsewhere. Something wasn't adding up. He closed his eyes and tapped his forehead with his index finger. *Toxinates love water. That's one reason the Red Toxinate was buried in a vault where there was no water. It was assumed that eventually the Toxinate would die. Obviously we were wrong.*

The Corporal walked up to the place where the water flowed through a one-foot opening into the building. The cement walls glistened with the water's spray and framed the large steel, horizontal doors holding back the river from flooding the building. The doors opened like a large mouth. Wider to let in more water, and narrower to let in less. He reached over the railing and put his hand in the opening. He let the cold water run through his fingers. He then ran his hand along the steel of the door where the water was flowing over, and scraped some of the slime build up off with his fingers. Bringing it up close to his eyes, he studied it.

Chief Ruther crouched beside him also trying to look at the slime under his fingernails. The Corporal looked out the corner of his eyes at the Chief bending a little too close.

"Did you find anything?"

The question sounded muffled in the sound of the water crashing into the tank. There was a stiff shake of his head, and the Corporal leaned in again, ran his hand down the inside of the steel wall, and again came up with some sludge. Again, he shook his head slightly, flung the excess mud into the pool, and wiped his hands on his army pants. He stepped away from the ledge and spoke loudly.

"Can we shut this door so we can stop the water flow?"

"What?" Ruther stepped closer.

"Can we shut this door," his hand gestured to the large steel door where the water was pouring through.

"I Can't Hear You!" Ruther shouted the words to indicate that the Corporal needed to speak louder.

Corporal James shook his head, turned towards the guard and motioned him out of the area.

Minutes later, the Corporal returned, the doors cranked shut, and Corporal again leaned up against the railing and focused on the inside of the wall. The quiet made every noise in the area sound that much louder.

"See that?"

The Corporal pointed to dime size glob of shiny Silver stuck to the inside of the steel door. Chief Ruther nodded and tried to not get distracted by the hair sticking out from the back of his collar.

"That's Silver Toxinate."

# Chapter Twenty Three

July 24<sup>th</sup>
Early afternoon

"How much further should we go?

Brooks and Dolan had been walking crouched for awhile and their necks were starting to get stiff. Dolan, the taller of the two, found it especially hard to continually stoop without being able to stretch.

Brooks continued, "If it knows we're here—then Brandon knows we are here too. Wouldn't it be safer to meet him on our terms?—Where we want to meet him, rather than in a place where he could have the advantage?"

Dolan stopped and sat down rubbing his neck.

"Lets' think this through, bro. You've got a point. We need to be able to escape; running while crouching is not going to work . . . we'll end up bashing our heads or something. Plus Brandon probably knows these tunnels far too well."

Dolan looked up to the roof.

"Have you seen a manhole recently?"

Brooks shook his head, "We've been slowly going deeper and deeper. I get the feeling that we're somewhere pretty remote under the city."

"So you just want to sit here and wait?"

"No. But I don't think we should keep going on blindly either."

"Do you think we could draw him out of these lit tunnels into one of these side tunnels where the Silver is not so intense?"

Brooks nodded, "That's the key."

Dolan always did the majority of planning for the two of them. They had grown up together in Highland Green. They had both attended G.H. Dawe Elementary school and both sporadically. Brooks wore black cords because Dolan did. He had them extra baggy, and walked on the bottoms so they were stripped to threads, because Dolan did. In all their escapades, Dolan was the one to get them into trouble but was also the one to get them out. This situation was no different. Brooks was the follower.

"So," Brooks looked at Dolan, "Do we turn around and find this *ideal* place you are talking about?"

Dolan looked ahead into the glowing tunnel. The tunnel got brighter and brighter like there was a silver sun waiting at the end. Dolan looked behind him. Tunnels constantly veered off at various angles and at various intersections.

Dolan opened his mouth to respond, when a loud scuffling sound echoed from ahead. Both boys looked at each other, eyes wide. Without a word they began to duck and work their way backwards. The sound of someone or something approaching was loud in the small space of the tunnels. The Silver on the walls glowed with greater intensity, and fear began to knot in their stomachs. Dolan and Brooks scooted back down the way they came, pausing and listening, hearts pounding and nerves on high alert. They rounded a couple corners until the tunnels were larger.

Stopping, they placed their hands on their knees and sucked in ragged breaths. The sounds of someone walking still echoed behind them. Heaving and wheezing, both boys calmed their burning lungs and took deep breaths to try to calm their nerves. Brooks stood up straight and looked at Dolan. Dolan nodded. They were at a T intersection. The lit tunnel they just came from ran straight and split into two directions. The left tunnel was darker than the right.

"Should we split up?" Brooks asked quietly.

"Yeah. It's the only way. Brandon will come down this tunnel to this intersection. He can't attack us both at the same time."

Brooks looked at the left hand tunnel, nodded and ducked around the corner into its darkness. Dolan moved into the right. Then they waited. The only sound was their breathing interrupted by the clunky footfalls of Brandon.

Brandon shuffled blankly through the tunnels. His steps were heavy and were being directed by the will of the source. His mind was blank. Void. He had become the perfect host. Silver danced and flowed all over him, while Red wove itself around him shimmering in anticipation. He was a glowing mass of light moving awkwardly through the tunnels. The Silver on the sides of the tunnel shimmered and danced. Each particle contributing to the mass effect, the same way a fan becomes a part of the crowd at a major football game.

Brandon plodded forward as he was instructed to do.

Brooks and Dolan didn't have to wait long. The Silver knew the tunnels, could sense their presence, and knew right where they were.

*I need a host,* the Red whispered in anticipation.

*I know.*

*It shall be yours.*

*May I . . . ,* The Red was moving like a python around Brandon's body, *I want to . . .*

*No.*

*Only I will control my host.*

*You will have your own soon enough.*

Dolan could see the whites of Brooks' eyes as he sat opposite of him crouched on the dried sludge. Brandon was right around the corner. Dolan's heart was pounding in his chest; he shakily stood to his feet.

Dolan shouted out, "Brandon it's me, Dolan. I'm around the corner."

Brooks went to yell as well, but Dolan quickly shook his head and put up his hand. Brooks closed his mouth and stayed crouched.

Again a bit of shuffling.

The source was thinking.

"Do you remember me? I'm Dolan, your friend." Dolan said the words slowly.

Suddenly, an electrical sound filled the air and a Silver spray hit the wall as if from a fire hose. The tunnel walls were soon coated in a thick layer of the substance. It overflowed into the tunnel where Dolan was crouched. Jumping back away from the wall, Dolan remained down in the centre of the tunnel and watched as the walls became a live glowing mass around him.

Dolan had the instinctive feeling that he was being trapped. He began to slowly move back, yet kept his eyes on the corner just ahead. He still hadn't seen Brandon. For some reason he was staying just around the corner.

"I'm your friend. Dolan. Remember the time we hung your sister's underwear from the clothes line and how mad she got at us? We laughed straight through till morning."

Dolan forced out a chuckle.

"Or the time Old man Chin caught us stealing in his store. He made us promise not to steal again. We promised and then walked out with candy still in our pockets. That was a hoot. You remembering this Brandon? Brandon? Brandon! Brandon . . . ?"

Dolans words vibrated the airwaves through the tunnel and were received by Brandon's ear. The message was sent immediately to his brain by his auditory nerve. The words sunk into his grey matter. His consciousness awoke. An unbidden memory floated into his mind's eye—underwear floating in the wind. This was funny. A small smile forced itself to his lips.

*Brandon . . . Brandon . . . Friend . . .*

How did he know these words?

Silver voices emerged and quickly tried to smash each nerve synapse in his brain. The words began to fade into the void again.

*It felt so good to think.*

Another thought. Another attack against the synapse.

The Silver was winding up like a tornado. This host was theirs and theirs alone.

*You will capture that boy.*

*I want him.*

The Silver's words rained like hail into his head and scrubbed away Brandon's emotions and thoughts. Brandon took another step forward and rounded the corner towards Dolan.

He raised both hands up in front of him holding a massive ball of swirling Silver.

Dolan, anticipating an attack of some sort, had moved back substantially. Silver swarmed all around him on the walls but he didn't touch it. He continued his barrage of words.

"I'm your friend. Listen to me. It's me, Dolan." "F-r-i-e-n-d, we're friends."

Were the memories strong enough? He needed to evoke more emotion. Dolan sorted through his mental index for the best, most emotional story.

Brandon rounded the corner and was standing in front of him.

"I know! Remember when we all went out looking for your dog, Lola? Remember Lola? You loved it when she lay across your lap when we watched movies at your house. You must remember that day . . . the day we found her on the side of the road after she was hit by a truck? We knelt down and carried her body back to the house? Or the time we kayaked at Turtle Lake? You hit a huge rock and I had to drag you and the kayak all the way back to shore? Remember this?

But Brandon was no longer listening.

He lifted up the ball of Silver, swirling and writhing like a ball of fire; casting splashes of light and sparks everywhere. Seeing Dolan stagger further back into the tunnel, Brandon flung out his hands and fired the swirling mass towards Dolan. The liquid Silver whipped through the air, electrifying the Silver splattered all along the walls as it streaked past.

Dolan stood. He watched. He turned and ran. Blasting through the tunnels, he could hear the whistling sound of the Silver. He could hear voices screaming at him in his mind. All around there was glowing Silver. He continued to run.

The flaming ball continued to gather speed.

Brooks sat spellbound. He watched Brandon as the shining ball of Silver chased after Dolan. *This is insane. Who are we trying to fool? We're way out of our league. I don't think Brandon has seen me yet . . .*

Brooks stood up and turned quietly to hide further down the tunnel. Maybe he could meet up with Dolan later—if there was a later . . . He took a few steps forward before he was driven to the ground by a pounding force that crashed into his back. His breath was driven from his lungs as he hit the ground. Gasping for breath, he lifted his head off the sludge.

The cool of the Silver seeped through his clothes. It swarmed over his body, pinning him under a glowing web to the ground of the tunnel. Brooks could only turn his head back and forth as he tried to get up, but the force of the Silver on his back was too much.

Voices, millions of small voices began to encourage him to lay still. The more Brooks tried to get up, the stronger the bonds became that cinched him to the floor. Brandon stood above him, eyes blank, hands out, Silver streaming from them onto Brooks. As the Silver hit Brooks, it swarmed and melded, forming a blanket with the glowing liquid.

Already Brooks could feel his thoughts clouding over. A chorus of voices, not his own were seeking to control his focus. With every fibre of his being, he narrowed his thoughts to Dolan. It was all he could do to focus on that one image. The second he thought of what was happening to his body, he began to lose control. The urge to fight, the panic, sent chemicals through his body that had to be controlled. He had to concentrate. This image of Dolan was his lifeline.

Brooks wanted to gag as the Silver crept up his neck and over his chin seeking his mouth. At the same time, it closed in over his ears enhancing all sound. His eyes burned cold as it forced itself under his eyelids. The violation caused Brooks to open his mouth to scream. The Silver swarmed immediately into the open cavity and down his throat. Brooks gasped. He felt completely helpless. He was slowly losing himself. His mind was an explosion of light. His lungs were flaming torches. His ears, a river of fire.

From above, Brandon watched stoically as the Silver swarmed around and claimed a new host. Brooks.

Brooks brought his mind back to Dolan, the last thought available in his brain. He saw him running from the swift ball of Silver. As the rest of Brook's body became covered with the Silver, he stopped straining and laid there with his face to the ground. His mind and memories were quickly drowned by Silver's voices. Brooks replayed the scene of Dolan running down the tunnel from the Silver—over and over and over again.

He was cocooned in a lumpy carpet of Silver . . . a hidden captive, a living host.

*Brandon flung out his hands and fired*
*the swirling mass towards Dolan.*

# Chapter Twenty Four

Dolan continued to run. Seeing another intersection in the tunnel ahead, Dolan ran straight ahead for the wall. The glowing ball was licking at his skin now and it was all he could do to keep ahead of it.

Blasting ahead, Dolan threw himself at the tunnel wall, curled up in ball and dropped. The impact with the cement jarred his body. He could feel his ribs bending inward, and there was a smack as his bruised flesh hit the floor. Moving quickly, he rolled back into a standing position and again began to run.

The ball of Silver hit the wall with a thunderous crack and the glowing ball burst like a water-filled balloon. Silver rained from the roof.

Dolan watched from a distance as the Silver slagged itself all over the tunnel walls.

"Hiya." Dolan leaned on his knees and caught his breath. He listened.

*There has to be a way to get Brandon to remember,* he thought to himself. His heart was pounding in his chest and his ribs hurt to breathe. His ankle ached from being in disuse for so long. Dolan listened. He couldn't see or hear Brandon coming down the tunnel.

Dolan looked up and squinted in the tunnel in hopes of seeing Brooks. Nothing. They shouldn't have separated. *I wonder if Brooks ran away when he saw me running.* Dolan rubbed his forehead into the heels of his hands. Talking to Brandon about memories wasn't enough. The pull somehow wasn't strong enough. They needed something stronger . . . something that he could see and touch . . .

Dolan continued to stand. There was Silver everywhere, but it was no threat as long as he didn't touch it. Even still, he needed to get out of the sewer system away from all the toxicity. He looked down the tunnel behind him and saw that light from the manholes was growing dimmer. Sunset was coming. He also needed to find Brooks. The last thing he wanted, was to be stuck down here alone, with the evil slime. He shivered. Finding Brooks had to be his first priority.

He started down the tunnel, retracing his steps back to the t-intersection where he had left his friend.

The walls glimmered brightly when he passed as if nodding at him, acknowledging his presence.

Brooks remained pinned to the floor. Voices clambered in his mind trying to gain control.

Though Brooks lay totally still, there was a war going on in his mind. He had to keep the thought of Dolan front and centre. He replayed the picture of Dolan running down the tunnel for his life repeatedly in his mind. All the while, the Silver kept pounding away at his defences. Brooks could feel it wanting access to his memories. Once, he had relaxed and begun to daydream. The Silver had quickly closed in. Immediately he slammed down his defences and refocused on Dolan. The mental fatigue was getting to him.

*How long can I keep my focus? What happens if I go to sleep?* Brooks knew he was in a fight for his life. The Silver wanted him. All of him. He wondered where Dolan was now . . . hopefully not in the same position he was in . . .

Brandon stood awaiting his next command. Silently and robotically he turned back the way he came and shuffled back into the glowing tunnels. The Silver's thirst had been quenched. It wouldn't have to wait long until the new host would be theirs.

When Dolan came upon the intersection, all was clear. Silver remained splattered everywhere but glowed with less intensity. Brooks was nowhere to be seen.

Stepping around a mass of glowing Silver on the floor, Dolan continued to walk down the tunnel—cautiously realizing that Brandon may launch another attack. After walking for about ten minutes while continually keeping an eye on the waning light from the manhole covers, Dolan saw no sign of Brooks, Brandon, or any sign of a fight.

Back at the intersection, Dolan knelt on the dry ground and tried to imagine what could have happened. One obvious conclusion was that Brooks had been captured and was with Brandon somewhere straight ahead. Not a good conclusion, but a plausible one. He looked around again. Silver was still everywhere, but . . . his eyes rested on the mound of Silver pulsating on the floor a couple of meters to the left of him.

Was that here before?

Dolan watched. The mound was pulsing, but was also swirling and diving and moving more rapidly than any of the stuff on the wall. It looked like the Silver that surrounded Brandon . . .

"Brooks!" Dolan leapt to his feet. "Brooks, are you under there? Brooks?"

A faint voice penetrated Brooks' mental defences. It sounded like . . . Dolan. He was so focused on the memories of Dolan and keeping at bay the Silver's control that at first he didn't notice the voice. Then like a piercing, saving light, Dolan's voice grew stronger overtaking the trillion little voices and shocked Brooks' mind into high gear.

*He's here.*

That one thought brought an explosion of hope into Brooks' being. The Silver voices scattered, his mind cleared and he was his own again.

*I'm still pinned down, I'm coated, he can't see me. I've gotta let him know that I'm here . . .* focusing all of his mental faculties on his feet, he attempted to lift them.

The weight of the Silver was heavy and immediately responded by pressing harder on his legs. Brooks tried again, with every fibre of his being he forced his right leg to move up—if only just an inch—and then collapsed again, hoping it was enough of a signal to Dolan.

Dolan stood above the swirling mass.

"Brooks?" he said again tentatively. He watched. A movement. A shift. It was enough.

Dolan looked around. There was nothing but curved walls, and hard, packed ground within the darkness. Dolan quickly shrugged off his backpack and tried to use it to scrape off the Silver away from the pulsating mound. The bag was too flimsy, and the Silver just slipped off of it.

Throwing his backpack to the side, Dolan whipped off his shirt and bound it around his hands. He stepped to the end of the Silver mound, and with his wrapped hands, he grabbed a handful of Silver and threw it against the wall. It hit, smacked and stuck to the wall. He grabbed another handful and another. Soon he could see the tips of a pair of shoes.

His head first . . . Dolan jumped to the other side and carefully, quickly removed the Silver from Brooks face and shoulders. *I hope his mind ain't gone. I hope he's is still there. He must be there. He must be there. I need him to be there.*

As his head and then his shoulders became uncovered, Dolan winced as he saw that Brooks' eyes were shut and his mouth was full of Silver, which was breathing for him. Instinctively, Dolan cried out, "No. You can't have him!" He threw the shirt around his hands to the ground and began vigorously scraping the Silver from his friend's face. Cradling Brooks' head in his lap, Dolan stuck his fingers into his mouth. "You won't. You won't have him." He flung more Silver up against the wall. "Brooks, I'm here. Wake up Brooks. I'm here." He lifted up an eyelid and peeled off a scale of Silver. Anger welled up in him. "Arrrragh!" Frustrated, he stood up, grabbed Brooks by the armpits and pulled him away from the Silver. He attacked the Silver still swarming on Brooks' body. Violently stepping on any puddles on the floor, flinging the stuff against the wall. Dolan paused and breathed.

"You will be Ok Brooks. Brooks, you gotta' fight man. Fight. I know you can hear me. Cough this stuff out of your lungs. Force yourself." With his last words an idea came into his head. He jumped down and turned Brooks onto his side. Looking at his fingers, he jammed them into Brooks' mouth and down his throat.

Immediately, Brooks began to gag. A stream of Silver began leaking out of his mouth, followed by globs as real air poured into his lungs. With a final crunch, Brooks threw his head forward and coughed up a puddle of Silver.

He opened his eyes and shut them. Dolan reached forward and placed his thumbs on Brooks' eyelids and smoothed them down. Silver squeezed out like puss from a pimple. Brooks lifted his hands to his face and blew out his nose onto the ground.

He opened his eyes and saw Dolan looking intensely at him. He went to speak and gagged. He spit and vomited up the last of the Silver in his mouth and lungs. Dolan stood up and took a step back. He wasn't sure what would happen next—he had to be ready for anything.

Brooks cleared his voice and said "Hey, took ya' long enough."

Dolan smiled big as relief poured over him.

"Yeah. Sorry man, let's get out of here, eh?"

Brandon lay unmoving in the narrowest part of the tunnel. His head lay up against a precipice, as he stared vacantly at the glowing ceiling above him. He felt nothing. He had no fear. He had no pain. His life had become a constant drone of voices now manipulating the body and mind that had once been his.

On top of him, the Silver and the Red spiralled in a sort of cosmic embrace. They were excited about their most recent capture.

Brandon didn't understand their triumph. He didn't need to. He was only a host. He closed his eyes and let another numbing sleep overtake him.

The whiplash vine of Red and the swirling puddle of Silver danced in a state of ecstasy around him. Their voices in harmony with each other. With slashes and spirals, splashes and snaps, the Red source shared its plans of hosting the new captive. The Silver source giggled and sparkled with delight. As they celebrated their victory, neither noticed the seeping loss of control over their new host.

# Chapter Twenty Five

Dolan looked at Brooks. He still had a slight shimmer to him.

"You are infected, you know that, eh?"

"No, I'm not."

"Yes, you are Brooks. I can see the shimmer around you. It was overtaking you. We'll have to find a way to disinfect you."

"I'm not."

Brooks stopped and physically turned Dolan to face him.

"I'm not infected. I'm not a host for that . . . that . . . evil, violent, rotten, puke smelling, friend stealing, glowing crap! And I'll tell you why. In order to become 'overtaken', you have to at some point give yourself to it. As long as you can hold onto at least one part of yourself, it can't use you for itself. It can only keep you captive. It starts off kind of nice, comes on with a cool feeling, soft voices and so on. It needs you to give it permission, so to speak."

Dolan's eyes were intense in the minimal light left in the tunnel, "Go on," he encouraged.

"I figured this all out," Brooks continued, "The stuff has a need to live off humans. It's useless as you can see around us on these walls. It can't do anything without us. It needs a mind. But it has to be a willing mind. Once it has that, it'll start to take control. This is where the memories fit in. The memories make us feel emotion. Emotion is hard to control. It comes from somewhere within you and not from your mind. This causes the Silver to lose its grip on a person. While I was laying there covered in the gunk, there wasn't a battle for my body. It was a battle for my mind. I was afraid that if I fell asleep it would take me, but I don't think it could've. I would've had to give it permission. This Silver was wearing me down. By sheer exhaustion I may have given in. Then, I would no longer be in control and it would have had me. But look at me."

Dolan did. He looked like the Brooks he had always known.

"I'm Brooks. Mind you, right now I can see crystal clear in this dark, and I could probably float like you did in water and maybe I could even breathe under water. But I'm in control of my mind. I'm in control of me."

Dolan whistled. "This is crazy. We are learning more—but still, I'd feel more comfortable hanging with you after you've had a bath in tomato soup or something."

"I haven't been sprayed by a skunk, you idiot."

"Well, maybe Coke then."

"Now you're talking."

They only walked a couple minutes when the sound of crying pierced Brooks' ears.

"What's that sound?"

"What sound? All I hear is your breathing down my neck."

"Seriously," Brooks stopped and listened intently. "Someone or something is crying up ahead."

Dolan also listened. "I don't hear a thing."

Brooks stuck a finger in his ear and scooped out a small amount of Silver. Flicked it on to a nearby wall like an unwanted wad of snot.

Dolan nodded, "Let's go see what it is then. No one else in their right mind should be down here, but us."

Dolan and Brooks ran ahead. After rounding a few turns, they saw a young girl sitting in the dark of the tunnels.

Her hands were wrapped around her knees, and she rocked back and forth, whimpering silently.

"You heard her crying?" Dolan whispered to Brooks.

Brooks nodded.

They both walked forward.

"Ah, hello?" Brooks spoke cautiously.

The young girl looked up and turned towards them. Dolan gasped and immediately ran to her.

"Carlee! What! What are you doing? Why are you here?"

Dolan grabbed her into his arms pulling her right off the ground. Carlee buried her head into his bare chest, her relief resulting in a new wave of tears. Dolan waited and then lifted her head gently up and wiped hair out of her eyes.

"What are you doing down here?" he asked again.

He was trying to keep the anger from his voice, but he wasn't doing a good job.

Carlee looked up at her older brother. He stank of sweat and mud. His brown eyes were shining like they always did. She looked deeper and instantly felt better, safer.

"Keenan and I . . ." she began.

"Keenan is down here too!?" Dolan shook her a bit.

"Keenan and I, we . . . uh . . . followed you and Brooks down here."

"Why would you do that?" Dolan looked at Brooks and he shrugged his shoulders.

"Keenan and I were there the day you were attacked on the bridge. We wanted to follow you to see what would happen."

"Sis, I wish you hadn't come down here. This is dangerous stuff."

He picked some mud out from her hair.

"Now why are you crying?"

Carlee pulled away and took a step back. She looked at Dolan, then at Brooks and back at Dolan. Grabbing her hair from behind her shoulders, she lifted it off her back and curled it up onto the top of her head as she sorted out her thoughts. Brooks noticed how thick her hair was, and then was suddenly embarrassed. Quickly, he averted his eyes.

"I don't know what this silver stuff is . . . I know it can hurt you somehow. I couldn't convince Keenan of that."

"What are you saying?" Dolan's eyebrows lifted slightly.

"Keenan took in the Silver," Carlee stated as she dropped her eyes to the floor, "I couldn't stop him."

"What do you mean by 'took it in'?" Dolan's voice raised a little.

"He took it in. He took some and rubbed it into his eyes. He let it go into him."

Carlee began to shiver as she recalled the look of ecstasy she had left Keenan in. "It wasn't right."

Dolan looked at Brooks and punched the meat of his fist against the wall. "Arrrr! Stupid. Stupid! What a stupid kid! Why would he do that? The idiot! Couldn't he see what happened to Brandon?"

"We'll get him back Dolan," Carlee placed a hand on his bicep. "I know."

"What do we do?" Carlee's voice fell to a whisper.

Brooks let out a long breath of air, "I don't know . . . he gave himself willingly to it. He followed what Brandon did."

He looked up at Dolan and glanced at Carlee.

Again, he couldn't help notice how pretty her eyes were. *Stupid, idiot, Butthead,* he scolded himself and looked down.

"Brooks, do you think he's lost like Brandon?" Carlee asked sincerely.

Brooks had no choice but to look straight into her deep, brown eyes, "I . . . uh . . . th . . ."

Dolan looked at Brooks with a worried glance. He turned to Carlee and stated, "No. No, not yet. There is time to save him still—but we have to find him first. It took Brandon a while I'm thinking to get completely overtaken. Brooks was completely covered in the stuff, and he's fine now."

"Yeah, but," Brooks answered, "I didn't willingly take it in."

"I know," Dolan shot Brooks a dirty look for scaring Carlee, "But still, it would take time to make him into a zombie like Brandon is." He turned again to Carlee, "Where did he go?"

"I don't know. I ran when I saw him take it in. I was scared. I didn't know what to do . . . oh Dolan . . . I don't want to lose Keenan . . . we can't let him be taken over . . . we can't."

Dolan looked at Brooks and they both took a step closer to Carlee. "We need to send you home sis. You shouldn't be here. This is a job for us guys."

Carlee's eyes grew defiant.

"I don't want to lose you too," Dolan added quickly.

"And I don't want to lose you. I'm coming." Carlee's look left no room for debate.

\*     \*     \*

Red roared violently in Brandon's mind. It whipped around Brandon binding him tighter and tighter. Brandon's dormant body jerked involuntarily with the Red's angry movements. *You lost the host. It's gone! You should've let me take him!*

The Silver Toxinate waited silently floating on top of Brandon's body until the Red calmed.

*There is another.*

*I feel him.*

Red paused.

*This one has already taken me and I am leading him here.*

Red relaxed into the Silver and listened to the rhythms she was feeling.

*Yes. There it is. This is unexpected. A willing host. I want this one.*

Silver answered, *This one is yours.*

*After all these years, I will finally have my revenge.*

Red settled onto Brandon's body and waited.

\*     \*     \*

The air was muggy from the heat of the day. Night was descending and families were settling in for the evening. Lights lit up rooms in run-down apartments above the downtown shops. Street lights flickered on, creating dark shadows in the alleys and in shop entrances.

Dolan, Brooks and Carlee walked back through the darkening streets of Downtown Red Deer. They had decided that they needed to return home and regroup. Finding Keenan in the darkness would be futile, and of course Brandon was still somewhere in the dark as well.

"What's our plan now?" asked Brooks.

"I think we should go down again," Dolan said slowly, "Prepared this time. We will need more supplies, shields of some sort, eyewear, and something, something to draw it out. We can't fight the Silver down there. There's too much of it and it's too enclosed for us."

"I think we should call the police," Carlee jumped in.

"Not yet. Soon. But not yet. We don't want Brandon shot remember? The police will shoot Brandon. They think he is a ghost or a menace."

"We'll tell them about the Silver and that Brandon's not a ghost," Carlee responded.

"Do you think they'll listen to you?" Dolan asked.

"They might." Surprised, Dolan and Carlee looked at Brooks.

"What did you say?"

Brooks responded to Dolan, "They might listen to Carlee."

Dolan shook his head and kept walking. Carlee looked over at Brooks from behind Dolan's back and smiled. Brooks nodded, smiled back, and kept walking.

# Chapter Twenty Six

Keenan walked further and further into the tunnel system. He was feeling powerful. His eyes were sharp and he saw every detail in the sewers. The initial rush of the Silver had subsided and left a cool feeling inside him.

He liked it.

He felt confident.

This was new. Keenan ran his hands along the sides of the tunnels as he walked. As Silver passed through his fingers, it crawled up his hands. Keenan stopped. The cool sensation was familiar and comforting. Soothing. He let it make its way up to his elbow, and then scooped some into the palm of his hand. He thought of Brandon and the authority he wielded on the bridge. He was holding power. Could he control it?

A voice whispered in his head.

*Yes you can. You are stronger. The other was weak. Take us in. Feel what it is like to be powerful.*

Keenan continued to stare, mesmerized by the glow and its sparkle. Shaking his head a bit, he tossed the stuff behind him and continued to walk forward. He had to think more about the possibilities.

He had to think.

# PART III

*Intoxinated*

# Chapter Twenty Seven

July 25<sup>th</sup>
Morning

Corporal James had an entire squad scouring the shores of the river. The men and women, who were recruits from the reserves and were dressed in their full army gear. The discovery of Silver Toxinate in the water treatment centre was a big step in the investigation. They had narrowed down the search to the riverbed. Now they had to find its den. They were getting closer—he could feel it. Standing on the bank at Three Mile Bend Park, looking down at his recruits dragging nets in the Red Deer River, he turned the facts over again in his mind.

The Silver was out there. It had found the Red. The Silver Toxinate and Red Toxinate were communicating somehow. They must, therefore, be somewhat similar in composition. Previous documentation reported only one Red Toxinate, and one Silver Toxinate. The Red Toxinate was taken out of seclusion in the army base and shipped here to Red Deer, Alberta. The Silver was never captured. It was elusive and yet left traces of itself. It somehow self replicated—the source of its replication was always hidden. No matter how much Silver they captured, there was always more. Silver Toxinate in the river meant Silver Toxinate in the treatment plant, as he had already discovered. Did this mean there was Silver Toxinate in the drinking water? Corporal James pushed the thought to the back of his mind. The implications of the type of infestation were too severe to dwell on. The potential for disaster was too real. Besides, the city seemed to have a very thorough water treatment program. Corporal James looked across the river to the opposite bank. His recruits were being thorough in their search—as they had been trained to do. They were good. But at this rate, they would be here all summer. *We need a break, some sort of hint or something to speed up the process.* Every day they didn't find the source of the Silver Toxinate was another day someone else might become infected. He reviewed his strategy for downtown. All the residents were alert, he had recruits stationed throughout the alleys in the city during the night. The last couple of nights had been quiet, but the Silver Toxinate would show itself again. And when it did, they would be ready. His men were ordered to shoot the individual on sight. Each officer in the detachment, each reserve recruit had been briefed on the danger of dealing with the Toxinate and what it could accomplish. Now, it was a waiting game. Corporal James recalled the coolness he felt when he scraped the Silver off the walls in the treatment centre. It was nice. It was not a menacing feeling. Then again, that was what the scientists had thought as well. The Corporal shook his head—*this stuff is more dangerous than we can imagine,* he thought to himself. *And where was the Red Toxinate in all of this? Had it taken a host yet?* The implications of both Toxinates in full control of a human had staggering possibilities. *We have no choice but to kill the hosts,* he thought again, *for the safety of the city—it's the only way.*

Chief Ruther noticed his head shake.

"Everything all right sir?"

The Corporal glanced at the police chief and nodded. "For now," he stated quietly, "For now."

\*     \*     \*

Brooks looked at Dolan shaking his head, "Everything all right?"

They were standing around the manhole looking down into its depths. It was early morning. Dolan, Brooks and Carlee formed a triangle. They were in this together.

Dolan looked across the manhole to his sister and Brooks and smiled.

They were covered from head to toe, complete with toques, rubber boots, as well as a backpack of supplies. Each of their backpacks sported a silver, galvanized garbage can lid. They looked like tiny fire fighters getting ready to put out a fire. They were as ready as they could be.

One by one, they lowered themselves into the now familiar tunnels. The moist, dank, air. The blackness, the bottom sludge, and the smells to go with it, washed over them as they dropped with a thunk to the bottom of the tunnel.

Brooks reached up, grabbed Carlee by the waist and lowered her down to the bottom. As soon as she felt her feet touch, Carlee let go of the rope. Brooks's hands lingered on her waist for a moment. Carlee brought her hands down to rest on his hands. Brooks eased his hands off her waist. Carlee's face flushed. She looked quickly down, her back still to Brooks, she began to absently brush dust from her fleece jacket. The lift down was surprisingly nice. Her waist still burned where Brooks hands had been. Brooks sunk his hands deep in his pockets and kicked his feet around in the muck.

Dolan was the last to climb down. He again tied a rope to the bottom rung of the 9-step iron ladder and slid down to the bottom. He looked at the two of them when he landed.

"Something up guys?"

"Nope," Brooks snapped his head up, smiled and said "Let's get down to business."

"Carlee, are you good to go?"

"I'm in," she replied softly. Being down in the dark again with the glowing Silver unnerved her.

"You both know the plan. We'll always meet here if something goes wrong."

Carlee and Brooks avoided looking at each other, and nodded.

None of them knew how wrong things would end up.

# Chapter Twenty Eight

20 minutes later

"This looks like the intersection," Brooks stated. The three of them stopped, dropped their packs, and began to proceed with the first stage of their plan. This was where they had first met Brandon. They didn't know if he would show up again or not. They had noticed that the Silver seemed aware of their presence. As they passed, it glowed brighter.

"This stuff knows we're here," Brooks stated as he stared at the Silver on the wall.

Dolan nodded, "I assumed as much."

"Do you think Keenan knows were here?" Carlee asked.

Dolan stopped and ran his hands over his shaved head.

"I don't know. He pretty much just disappeared last night. I think we're going to have to expect the worst. Knowing what we know, the Silver may have him brain fried as well—but maybe not to the same degree. I'm hoping that seeing the two of us," he gestured to Carlee, "That we'll be his memories. He's our brother . . . he knows us."

Carlee nodded, "I agree. Dolan?"

He nodded, indicating that he was listening, "We don't leave here without him, Ok?"

"Ok."

Brandon's house had been empty and unlocked as usual. It had been easy to take a few items. They left a note on the dirty kitchen table that stated they were there and then left.

Working quickly now, they opened Carlee's backpack and dropped off the items they had taken. A pair of jeans, a Tu Pac CD, and a DCSHOECO t-shirt. Leaving a small pile, they headed back the way they came.

They retraced their steps down the tunnel and left another small pile of items. This time, it was a pillow from his bed, a ragged and stuffed monkey with a red, hand sewn outfit, and his flannel Spiderman pj's that were at least three sizes too small.

"Do you think he'll remember these?" Brooks wondered aloud.

"I guess we'll see, eh?" said Dolan, "Come on, we have one more drop off."

They walked to the bottom of the manhole where the rope hung down like a lonely snake hanging from a tree. Here, they dropped off some pictures. A pile of pictures. Pictures that Brandon's mom had never bothered to put into albums. Pictures of Brandon being held as a baby, pictures of their school trip to the mountains, pictures of the girl he used to like named Renee. They worked quickly and stuck them on the wall with the muck from under their feet.

"Ok, this is it." Dolan wiped the gunk from his fingers on his black pants leaving a long brown stain. "Now we have to provoke this glowing snot into action!"

Carlee and Brooks grinned and got to work

The three of them put on rubber gloves they took from under the kitchen sink. They were truly a sight. Walking down the tunnel, they began to sweep the Silver off the walls and into large garbage bags.

At first they found it to be kinda' fun. Brooks started by grabbing a swath and slamming it into his garbage bag like a slam-dunk.

"Hey that's snot mine, it's yours!" Dolan and Carlee howled with laughter. Their laughs echoed down the tunnels and faded.

"Look a hole in one!" Brooks called as he tossed some into Carlee's garbage bag.

"Oh go fling your snot somewhere else!"

"Look out, here is my slam gunk!"

Together the three of them laughed and mocked the Silver as they filled their bags with it. Their laughter helped them to feel the confidence that they didn't really have. After a while, the jokes diminished. The three of them continued to work, each lost in their own silent thoughts. Each listening intently for a sound from either Brandon and Keenan.

\* \* \*

Keenan sat cross-legged beside Brandon, who now lay comatose on the floor. The Silver Toxinate swirled and danced around him. His eyes were vacant.

Keenan was different. Keenan's eyes weren't vacant. In his hands, he held what looked like a tightly bound ball of red string. A voice clambered around his head seeking to be heard. Keenan ignored it—for the time being. He mentally reviewed how he got here.

After he took in the Silver, and Carlee had ran off—he felt alive and powerful. He had walked for a while bathing in the rush of his feelings. Eventually, the voice had led him here. It constantly invited him to indulge in more of the Silver, to feel its coolness, to allow it to be a part of him. Keenan ignored the voice for the most part. He held on to the picture of Brandon. Of him losing control and then just about killing Brooks and Dolan on the bridge.

Yet, here he was. He was sitting beside Brandon. Keenan looked at Brandon and wondered again if he was even still alive. He looked so, so . . . not himself. The Red whipping 'stuff' had been weaving around Brandon as a chain wraps around a log about to lifted onto a logging truck. Now that chain was in his hands.

It was the voice of the Red that cried out the loudest to Keenan. The intense, insistent, and strong voice commanded his attention and finally, he gave it. In his mind, Keenan had negotiated with the Red. They had come to a mutual sort of understanding. Keenan would play host, and the Red would obey his wishes. The Red needed a host, and Keenan needed the power. A thought of his mother's boyfriend, Brad, bound with Red to the floor and suffocating brought a smile to his lips. Too long had Keenan felt helpless at the hands of his mother's abusive boyfriends. Too long had he born the brunt of their alcoholic rages. Now, it would be his turn. His faced flushed as he remembered whimpering in his and Carlee's room in fear of what Brad would do next. It was a life of weekends lived in fear. One after the other. Not anymore.

Red had screamed at first. A silent scream only the thoughts could hear. It felt there was no need to negotiate. It would simply take Keenan's mind by force. There was a battle that ensued as Red violently attempted to gain control. Yet Keenan kept his mind and body still. He cringed as the Red Toxinate wrapped itself around his head and began to battle, but kept still. The Red Toxinate threw itself against Keenan's mind seeking to demolish memories and instill fear. Keenan remained still and chose not to engage. Throwing up mental blockades had been simple enough and he merely waited out the onslaught. And then, as suddenly as it had started, it stopped. The pounding on his mind's walls finished and the attempt to control subsided. The Red Toxinate slipped from around his head and dropped into his hands. A voice spoke into his mind, *I will allow you to use me.* Keenan grabbed the rest of the Red dangling from Brandon's body and pulled. Quickly, a whip of Red unfurled and waved like fly-fishing string from Keenan's hand. He sat fascinated. The Red Toxinate natural form was like a snake. It shimmered and was constantly in motion. Yet it was fluid enough to be reshaped to fulfill an intended purpose. Keenan let his mind enter into the Red. He was immediately accosted with intense hatred. He withdrew. The life form was violent, and he could feel its need to release pent-up energy. It dawned on Keenan why it needed a host. Without the host, himself, the power was useless and contained. The life form, this red glowing liquid snake, needed feet to transport it, hands to mould it, and thoughts to facilitate its desires of vengeance.

He let his mind open up and allowed the Red to partially enter, but only so far. With ease, he shut it down and watched the Red slither out of his thoughts like a snake being chased out of a house. Keenan then tried to probe the Red. As their thoughts collided in force, Keenan pushed deeper into the makeup of this life form. He felt its raw instinct to stay alive and to devour. He could feel the heat of its anger—violent, impulsive, thirsty. He was bombarded with flashes of colour, red mostly—in varying shades and intensities. Within the tumult of colour, there were small pockets of blackness. It was these pockets of blackness that caught his attention. Keenan pushed in further. It was at this point that the Red fought him with a ferociousness that left him trembling. Swiftly, he withdrew. Opening his eyes, he looked over at Brandon again and then down at his hands enmeshed in liquid Red.

He was playing with fire.

Brandon was gone. Burnt. He felt it. The source had claimed his mind and there was nothing left. Brandon didn't even know he was here beside him. The same could happen to him if he wasn't careful.


Crawling back down the tunnel, Keenan finally came to a place where he could stand straight up.

*What can you do?* He wondered.

He allowed the Red to communicate with him mentally, **Whatever I desire**, it replied icily.

"Or whatever I desire," Keenan said aloud.

With that, Keenan whipped out the Red into the rock walls of the tunnel. He sent out a command. Within seconds, it formed a picture of a horse on the wall. The Red screamed in anger at being used so frivolously. Keenan smiled and the Red flew off the wall and returned to his hands. This time, Keenan rolled the Red into a ball and dropped it to the ground. It bounced back to his hand. Keenan smiled again. With this type of ball, he could score a basket every time.

He felt a knock on his mind. He opened.

**Allow me.**

Keenan did.

His hands began to work on their own accord. They pounded the Red back and forth against the palms of his hands and stretched it out like a sheet in front of his face. Keenan's mouth opened, and he breathed hard into the sheet of Red. Instantly, the Red formed a small balloon shape and cloaked itself around like a glove over both of his hands.

**Punch the wall.**

Keenan walked to the tunnel wall and without hesitation, punched it hard with his fist.

SMASH! The air around him shuddered.

The wall crumbled around his arm, as his fist sunk deep into the cement. Slowly he withdrew his arm. The Red glowed as if it was on fire. His fists felt cool. He unwrapped the Red and looked at his knuckles. Brown as usual.

No pain.

Keenan sat down. The implications of what had just happened sent the possibilities tumbling and reeling. He was starting to feel hungry.

# Chapter Twenty Nine

Voices, and signals passed from the Toxinate and eventually to Brandon. The source pounded inside Brandon's head. With jerky movements, Brandon's body was manipulated into a standing position.

Keenan jerked his head up at the same time. He heard the distress signals as well. Faintly, but he heard them. He allowed the Red to communicate. Concentrating, he listened to the Red's voice, **They're** *raping us, stealing us, they'll ab-u-u-u-use.*

The usual anger and violence was there, but there was a subtle pain beneath it all. *What are they talking about? How could they be abused? They control others—who is the abuser here?* Keenan tried to listen again and probed deeper into the Red's thoughts.

*They'll hurt us. They used us before, tore us apart, experimented on us . . .* Keenan watched the whirlpools of colour . . . *help us. Stop them.*

Experimented on them?

Keenan pushed further to try to discover more. He aimed his thoughts towards the black holes always careful not to lose contact with himself. The Red coiled and spun in his hands, binding and loosening, whipping and falling . . . Keenan moved closer. The whirlpool spun faster, the black holes were elusive. Keenan edged even closer, still sending out a tendril of thought to penetrate into the black hole.

Immediately upon entry, the maelstrom stopped. Red spoke to him by formulating pictures with his imagination. He had entered a memory. Keenan saw Red caged in a white box in a vault, he saw the dimness of the red light, he saw lab coats, chemicals . . . the picture switched . . . he saw a mess. Blood splattered the room and pooled around the neck of a lab technician laying on the floor, Red was strangled around that neck and there were lacerations across the body . . . another picture . . . the vault . . . the white cage . . . screams and screams and screams and screams . . . a small door slams shut . . . silence.

Keenan withdrew slowly. He was breathing heavily.

The Red lay now limp in his hands.

"Thank you."

The Red curled around his hands and squeezed.

Brandon was standing beside him now, staring vacantly as usual while awaiting his next command. Keenan stood up, looked at the hole in the wall where his fist had gone through, and then followed Brandon down the tunnel.

*     *     *

After twenty minutes of 'snot-slinging', Brooks stood up straight and listened.

"Someone is coming," he said abruptly.

Carlee and Dolan stopped and looked at Brooks.

"You sure?" Dolan's voice carried with it an edge of excitement.

"Yes."

"All right guys, this is it. Let's pack these bags to the manhole opening."

"Do you really think this'll work?" Carlee lifted her bag of Silver up off the ground.

"Oh yeah. We're stopping the Silver spies from tracking us, plus it'll be safer for us without this stuff available to attack us."

They began to heft the loaded garbage bags back to the entry point. When they reached the entrance, Brooks and Carlee climbed up the rope and onto the rungs of the ladder.

"What are we going to do with all the Silver?" Brooks called down to Dolan.

Dolan looked up. The sunlight fell through the hole, lighting up Brooks like an angel from Heaven. Squinting his eyes, he called back, "We'll stick to the plan. You two be waiting up there and I'll draw him up. I'm just going to dump this stuff a ways around the corner."

Dolan lifted up all three bags with both hands and began to carry them away from the manhole opening. Sweat beaded, dripped, beaded, and dripped off his forehead. Three times, Dolan had to stop to set the bags on the wet floor of the tunnel in order to give his hands and arms a break. Still he continued on. He knew he didn't have much time. His garbage can lid swung back and forth across his back as he stumbled in the darkness.

Finally, he stopped. Carefully, he tied a knot in each bag and piled them up against the wall. The garbage bags glowed softly in the dark, the Silver's glow muffled by the darkness of the bags.

Running back to the manhole where the rope dangled down, Dolan, breathing heavily, began to drag himself up the rope. He paused, clutching the bottom rung to catch his breath. He could see Brooks and Carlee sitting at the edge, their back to the manhole.

Guarding it no doubt.

Whoosh!

A ball of Silver smashed into Dolan's side, throwing him off the rung and driving him to the floor. Dolan stumbled up, gasping at the pain in his ribs. Frantically, he wiped the Silver off his body. He felt it crawling like insects all over his body. He looked up and saw Brandon walking stone-like towards him. Another ball of Silver was forming in his hands. Dolan swung his garbage can lid in front of him, crying out in pain with the movement. He backed up slowly. Each step sent jagged pains into his lungs, and he wondered if his ribs might be cracked.

Brandon raised his hands. A flash of red caught Dolan's eye. His mouth dropped. It was then he saw Keenan behind Brandon. Dolan's mind did not have time to comprehend the implications, as the red whip snapped through the air.

*     *     *

Brandon had walked past the first pile of clothing, without even a pause. Keenan, was surprised to see the pile of stuff, but knew that Brandon wouldn't be interested. Brandon, the Brandon he knew, wasn't in that body as far as he could tell. Keenan had even tried to reach out to Brandon's mind, but found nothing there except for the whispering voice of the seductive Silver.

Keenan was still hungry though. He stopped to look through the clothes. They were damp from laying in the mud. No food. His stomach rumbling, he tracked after Brandon. At the second pile of stuff, Brandon again walked by without even looking down. Keenan stopped to search the old pj's and pillow for food. Nothing.

*Obviously, Brooks and Dolan had come back*, he thought.

Turning the last corner, Keenan saw a flash of silver. He saw Dolan crash to the ground. "What the . . . ?" Keenan muttered as he tried to make sense of the scene before him. At first Keenan stood stunned. Brandon stood, eerily still, until slowly he raised his hands. Dolan staggered backwards clutching his side. Brandon's hands rotated in a clockwise motion gathering more and more Silver. From all over his body, Silver streamed into his hands. The Silver grew into a glowing ball as if Brandon now wielded the sun. The glow intensified into a piercing Silver light. Keenan saw Dolan lift his arm to cover his eyes.

Keenan was suddenly jolted as the Red spoke to him with insistent urgency. It demanded that Keenan join in the fight. So he did. Keenan whisked out the Red Toxinate and sent it straight at Brandon. He commanded the Red to bind Brandon's arms tightly to his side. The Red was quickly lashed around Brandon and wound tightly, bringing his arms closer to his chest. This unexpected intrusion caused the ball of Silver to career wildly and hit the ceiling of the tunnel, raining onto the floor like a shower of Silver bullets.

Then unexpectedly, with a jolt, the Red cord slipped right off Brandon and fell uselessly to the floor. Keenan looked at it and opened up the communication. The Red was screaming and violent.

*No. No. You cannot use me against myself. Our powers are negligent against each other. You waste us and abuse our strength. Kill the boy!*

The words came muddled amidst a tirade of emotions.

The Red gathered itself back into Keenan's hands and shouted *Kill him!*

Looking down the tunnel, Keenan could see Dolan stepping backwards, garbage can lid raised and looking for a way out.

# Chapter Thirty

Dolan saw what happened. He saw how his brother wielded the Red with ease. A pang of guilt and fear settled deep inside.

*I should've been watching out for him. He should've been more careful about coming down here. Is he gone like Brandon? Was that an attack on Brandon? Who's in control?*

All Dolan knew was that he was no longer safe here. He backed away gingerly, carefully minding his aching side.

He could hear Brooks calling to him, "Where are you? Are you coming? Hurry up!"

He flicked his eyes up to the manhole opening, now a good ten feet in front of him. He continued to back up. Beads of sweat formed along his hairline and trickled down his cheeks. He felt vulnerable—a horrible feeling.

"Keenan!"

He saw his brother's head look towards him.

"Keenan, it's me. Dolan. I'm hurt, Keenan. I can't fight like this. Help me Keenan."

He was taking a chance he knew. Letting the enemy know your weakness wasn't always the best tactic. However, if Keenan wasn't totally gone, an emotion might be the saving grace.

Keenan heard Dolan's voice clear as a bell. He could hear every inflection and the fear wavering on the edge of every word. He had never known Dolan to show fear. A feeling of devotion shimmered through Keenan and he allowed it to grow. This was his brother.

The Red was now pounding against the walls of his mind. Shrieking to be heard. Keenan held it at bay a little longer. He was in control here. Even his brother Dolan wasn't in control. A wave of power surged through him. He was the one in control.

He looked up and saw Brandon walking forward with his zombie like gait. Brandon had lost control. The sense of playing with fire tickled at the edge of his mind. Keenan dropped his guard a bit. Red flooded in. **Use me. Destroy the boy. He will destroy us if you don't.** The Silver wanted Dolan dead as well.

*It is us or him,* the Silver whispered into his mind, *we must kill him. We want his blood today.*

Keenan was torn. His hunger for power was strong, but at what price? At the expense of his own flesh and blood? He couldn't do it. No. He was in control. He would make the decisions here.

So he did. Taking the Red, he rolled it into a ball, not unlike what Brandon was doing. He dashed ahead and sent it smashing into the side of the tunnel. Cement crumbled and blew out of the wall, as the Red left a large hole. Dust filled the air, clouding their vision.

Brandon stopped. Rubble lay scattered in front of them. Huge chucks of cement with rebar curving out of them like TV antennas littered the floor.

Keenan looked at the devastation he had just caused and blinked the dust out of his eyes.

Red spoke again, giggling sardonically, **Well done my faithful servant. Doesn't that feel good?**

Keenan blinked. It did feel good. Power felt good. He let the Red in a little more, enjoying the feeling. Unexpectedly, his hand jerked out and the Red flew through the air as a whip. It slammed down on the garbage can lid Dolan was holding. The lid sliced right in two and dropped to the ground. Blood splattered on the lid, its smell sending the Red into a frenzy.

Dolan cried out as the Red unexpectedly slammed into him. He held onto the garbage can lid just as the Red whip sliced cleanly through and snapped back, the whip just grazing his four fingers. The razor like cut split the lid in half. One half lay on the floor of the tunnel, and the other half was still clenched in his fist. Blood was running down his hands and dripping onto the floor.

Dolan looked up in fear and shouted, "Keenan! It's me! Your brother! Stop Brandon. We are here to save you, to help you . . . not to hurt you."

He looked from Keenan to Brandon. The rubble was a small deterrent, but not much. He didn't understand; it was almost as if Keenan tried to help him and in the same breath tried to kill him.

"Keenan!"

A shadow fell across the elongated circle of light on the tunnel floor. First feet and then a body appeared on the ladder rung.

"Dolan, are you all right?" Brooks' voice broke the lull.

"Climb back up!" Dolan called back, his breathing ragged from his surely broken ribs. He stole a look to Brandon once more . . . he was walking closer.

Keenan just stood. Frozen.

He could see Brooks scanning the darkness for a sign of Dolan. He was squinting while his eyes adjusted, and still had not seen Brandon.

"Look behind you, it's Brandon. Get out of here!" Dolan knew he had to make the best of this distraction, despite the danger that

Brooks was in. He saw Brooks turn around and begin to climb back up. Dolan continued to back up in the darkness of the tunnel. Farther and farther he stumbled. The last thing he saw was a photograph from the wall falling like a feather to the floor. He came to a corner in the tunnel and then disappeared from sight.

Sweat made Brooks' hands slippery as he tried to hurry back up the rungs. Carlee looked down to him, worry creasing her face. Desperately he climbed higher, trying to get out before Brandon saw him, but at the same time trying to lead him out into the daylight.

Brandon came to the pictures in the tunnel and paused. His eyes flitted disinterestedly over the pictures. His whole body glowed Silver and sparked electrically. Brooks paused on the rungs and watched.

"Brandon—it's me, Brooks."

Brandon didn't respond.

Climbing higher, Brooks pulled himself over the edge of the manhole and gave Carlee a quick smile. He laid down on his stomach and called again.

"Brandon, we're up here!"

This time Brandon did respond.

Keenan remained stationary. His eyes didn't blink, but the rise in his chest was constant and slight, indicating the continual drawing and expelling of air. About him, the Red Toxinate circled. Loosely at first and then tighter.

Keenan vaguely felt his face flush as the air was squeezed out of him. He was only slightly aware when the Red abruptly fell limply to the floor. He breathed in deeply and felt the process begin again. He felt the Red Toxinate climb up his body, wind itself and squeeze again, then as before, fall limply to the floor. Yet this was merely a representation of the larger battle raging inside. Swirls of Red bashed and battered against the strongholds of his mind. Keenan was slowly losing ground. The Red had a foothold in his mind. It was in too far. Keenan felt the Red's triumph and fought even harder to block his mind and to regain that which he had lost. The furious battle raged on. At times Keenan felt he was being squeezed in a vice and that his mind was going to explode. The Red lashed out again and again, binding, squeezing, gaining ground. Fatigue began to spread through Keenan's limbs. His legs began to quiver and he crumpled to the ground. The violent struggle intensified. The Red was like a tidal wave slamming against his mental defences and seeping in under the doors. Keenan was losing. He felt it. He had played with fire and had gotten burnt. The Red felt him weakening and this only spurred on its attack. The Red swirled and swirled around him. It flowed over Keenan's thoughts and memories like lava. This is what I am becoming, Keenan thought. He was now backed into a corner standing on the plot of memories left that he was in control of. Waves of Red sloshed on the shore where he stood, taking with it sands of himself back into its own red sea. Then an idea slid cautiously across that small portion of Keenan's mind that remained his. Gazing deeply into the Red, he saw the black holes he had entered previously. There they were. It was a desperate move. If he was unsuccessful, he would lose control of his own mind, but he was on the brink of losing control anyways. His small island wouldn't hold out for long. Maybe he could save a bit of himself and . . . and . . . he didn't know what would happened after that. Keenan gathered what mental strength he had left and dove for a black hole swirling past. Keenan immediately lost touch with himself and was sucked into the swirling vortex, the black hole—officially giving over control of his body.

Brandon looked up. He looked back at the pictures on the wall. A tenuous thread of recognition, as delicate as a line of spider's silk, floated to just beneath the surface of his mind. It bumped against the barrier of Silver. Thoughts like fish trying to stick their head out of the water in the middle of winter and only hitting ice weakly looked for a crack. Brandon's eyes skittered across each picture. Each picture evoking a memory. Each memory floating and lying against the frozen silver surface. The Silver laughed, still in complete control. It took Brandon's hands and forcefully ripped each picture to shreds.

It turned his head upwards. The Silver, swirling in Brandon's eyes, locked in on Brooks. With a quick fluid motion Brandon made a Silver rope and slung it on the rungs. Brandon's intoxinated blood boiled in anticipation of the upcoming confrontation. The Silver was hungry. It needed to feed. Brandon began to climb up out of the tunnels.

# Chapter Thirty One

1:18 pm

Brandon's mom picked up the phone and dialled.

"Red Deer RCMP detachment. How may I direct your call?"

"Hello. Yes, uh, this is Kendra. Kendra Spencer."

"Is that your legal name?"

"Yes." The question threw her off.

"What is it you are calling about?"

"Uh, my son is the one that is missing, Brandon Spencer? Have there been any leads or any information on where he could be?"

"Let me check his file. One moment please."

"No ma'am. Nothing has been added to his file in the last few days. With the downtown being in a state of emergency . . . well it's been tough to focus on the other cases."

"I understand. It's just that I think I may have some information that may help."

"Go ahead Ms. Spencer."

"Yes. Well, his friends came over this morning and took a bunch of stuff from his room. They left a note. At first I didn't think too much of it, but now I'm starting to wonder."

"What do you believe was taken?"

"Well, they took his pj's (an old pair), a pillow, photographs of his family and friends, clothing and some music. It is almost as if they are hiding him out somewhere and not telling me. I don't know why . . ."

"And the note . . ."

"Yes there was a note."

"And it said . . ."

"That they had been there, grabbed a few things and left."

"Who are 'they'?"

"Brooks and Dolan—his friends."

"I'll need specific names Ma'am."

"Right. Uh . . . Brooks Strawberry, Dolan Hawkeye."

"Where do they live, Kendra?"

"I don't really know for sure—uh, somewhere here on the north side. They all go to GH Dawe."

"Would you like an officer to come by the house and take a statement?"

Kendra sighed. "I would like my son to be found, but if a statement is all that can happen at the moment . . ."

"We're doing our best. Any information will help the investigation."

"I know . . . Yes, if an officer could come down . . . actually . . . I'm wondering if the boys actually know where Brandon is and are bringing him things. If we can find the boys, maybe we'll find my son?"

"That could very well be, ma'am. We'll have an officer see you within the hour."

"Thank you."

"I hope they find him soon, Ms. Spencer."

"I hope they find him soon too."

\*       \*       \*

Dolan continued to scramble away from the danger. His breathing became more ragged. Finally he stopped and leaned up against the tunnel wall to catch his breath. He listened. Footsteps. He was being followed. Holding his side, he pushed himself off the wall and continued to stagger forward praying that he would soon find some way out.

Keenan's body walked forward. The Red was fully in control now. Using Keenan, it lashed out at the tunnel walls shattering rock and cement everywhere. The Red Toxinate was now in its full element. A body, a host to control, and violence to inflict. Red let its anger vent itself on everything around and used Keenan's voice to laugh in mockery. Now in control of Keenan's thoughts and memories it was focusing on its next target.

"Dolan!"

Keenan's voice bounced off the wall and stopped Dolan in his tracks.

"Dolan, wait."

Dolan stopped. Something was off.

Keenan's voice sounded again, "I'm hungry!"

A chill crept up Dolan's spine. The word 'hungry' floated in the air around Dolan. Regret weighed heavily on his shoulders as he realized that Keenan was no longer Keenan. He stayed silent and continued to search for a place to hide.

A few minutes later, Keenan's voice again rebounded down the tunnel. Keenan's voice. Dolan winced. It was closer than he anticipated.

Dolan came to the bags of Silver that they had collected and crouched behind them. It wasn't much cover, but maybe enough to give him the element of surprise. He sat down, pulled off his backpack and looked for something, anything that he could use.

Seconds ticked by.

Dolan focused on controlling his breath. Looking down the tunnel, he could see Keenan. Red flashed all around him, slashing the walls and leaving crumbled cement all around him. Keenan walked robotically, stiffly, his voice occasionally bursting out in a stream of violent laughter.

*This is all my fault. Who else will I lose to all of this?* Dolan's guilt was clouding his thoughts. He had always been able to handle situations even at mom's parties—and those could get bad. His shoulders slumped as he realized this was beyond what he could handle. He sat and breathed slowly, trying to stay in control.

The Red Toxinate was in its glory. After years of imprisonment, it could finally exact the pound of flesh it dreamed about. Which pound of flesh it exacted was of no consequence. All humans were its enemy. Red continued to whip and destroy. It used Keenan's body to destroy and wreak destruction. It savoured the blood that was bleeding from the various lacerations it inflicted on Keenan's body. There was a life in the blood that was intoxicating. The Red fed off it. Craved it. Laughing with Keenan's voice and stretching his vocal chords to capacity, it readied itself for the kill.

Dolan looked one more time for anything that could help him. His eyes scanned the dark tunnel, his only escape. There wasn't much Silver clinging to the walls in this section. Small traces here and there, but that was it. The darkness was broken only by the occasional sunbeam, which filtered through the manhole covers found sporadically throughout the city. The floor was sticky and muddy, but not deep in sludge. Dolan's eyes ran up the smooth cement walls . . . he was . . . trapped. A vision of being slashed open by the Red filled his brain. He quickly let it go and focused his attention on Keenan, now getting closer.

Within his mind, Keenan tumbled and turned in the black abyss. He had lost his bearings and sense of direction. He searched for a way to stabilize himself, but the Red's fury seemed like a neverending siege. Keenan couldn't grasp any of the chaotic memories whizzing in and out of its consciousness.

If he could just get one . . . that was it. Just one.

Desperately he had taken this chance. He had thought it was the only way to save a small part of himself from the Red and to figure out a way to get control of himself again. Time did not matter here. Keenan was diminished to something like a thought. Like a thread of a ghost swirling in a world that was once his. Keenan's mind was only vaguely connected with his own body. A body in pain. A body inflicting indeterminate destruction.

Another memory whipped by and slipped from his grasp. Keenan dove and twisted and turned desperately trying to clutch a memory—any memory. He knew this was the only way to regain control of his own body. Before long he would be a permanent zombie—acting only to serve the Red. Suddenly, as another thought swirled close, Keenan felt a pull and was sucked through a filmy boundary.

The swirling stopped.

He was in. He was inside a memory of the Red Toxinate. He was intruding.

Keenan looked around.

All around him was craggy, grey rock. Rutted. Full of caverns. Keenan floated over them like a spirit. There were no shadows.

*Where in the world is this place?*

He floated some more. There seemed to be no life here. Nothing. Yet there had to be. The Red was here somewhere. He continued to float over the vast sea of grey rock. The undulating formations emphasized the rough unevenness of the ground below.

And then he saw it. A soft glow of red up ahead, behind a rock up-cropping. Keenan floated closer and up over the rock. He looked down at the source of the glow and his eyes widened in surprise.

The Red knew immediately that he had been violated. When Keenan had entered his memory, it proved that it had not been successful in taking all of him. The pain of Keenan entering that memory was intense. He thrashed Keenan's body to the ground. Keenan's hands ripped at his clothing, tearing his shirt to shreds. Yet the pain remained, like someone drilling a hole into its soul.

Dolan crouched, stunned by the scene in front of him. The Red was now only twenty feet in front of him, thrashing Keenan's body on the ground. Frightened, Dolan couldn't move. He continued to crouch and breathe and watch.

# Chapter Thirty Two

Ding. The old doorbell let out its rusty ring. The police had arrived at Brandon's home. Kendra answered the door and ushered in the police.

"Ma'am." The first officer in the door, was a skinny man with a thin moustache.

His small eyes continuously scanned the area around him. "There aren't many officers available these days. With the Silver Phantom on the loose, we have a lot of men tied up investigating sightings and reports. However, I can take down your report and we will file it." Kendra put out her smoke and plopped into a kitchen chair.

"You don't understand," she said dejectedly, "My son is out there. These kids are harbouring him. We could find him and bring him home."

She traced the grains in the wooden table with her index finger. The second officer, bald on top with hands clasped behind his back, cleared his throat and rocked up onto this toes and down again. He crinkled his nose at the dirty house and the heavy smell of cigarette smoke sticking to him.

"Ma'am," his voice husky and flat as he spoke, "Give us all the information you can and we'll keep our eyes open for these kids you've mentioned. It's the best we can offer at this time."

"We'll even do a quick drive-through in the area to see what we can see," the skinny one added and took out a pad of paper and a pencil.

"So describe these 'friends' of your son to me . . ."

*     *     *

Outside in the afternoon sun Carlee and Brooks backed away as Brandon climbed up out of the tunnel. They looked at each other apprehensively.

"Do you think the pictures did anything?" Carlee looked at Brooks in worry.

"I don't think they did a thing. You saw how he ripped them up."

They had backed away from the manhole until they reached a row of nearby trees. Their garbage can lids held tightly in their hands shielding their bodies.

They waited.

Brandon's glowing form emerged from the manhole eerily, blinding any who happened to glance his way. His feet rested on the ground, knees locked, and his stance awaiting command. His silver body was shimmering fluidly like heat waves in a desert. His once red hair was lined with silver. His eyes scanned the surroundings and quickly he found them. Easily, he formed the Silver into a long sword, lethal and pointed, and walked towards them.

Brooks made eye contact with Brandon's silver eyes. Fear began to jolt up and down through his spine. Thoughts of choking on the Silver rose in his memory. He searched for Brandon in those eyes, but saw only Silver. Adrenaline pumping, Brooks jumped forward, dropping his garbage can lid and throwing both hands into the air. He shouted, "Brandon, it's me! Brooks! I'm here to help you Brandon, you have to *trust* me."

Brandon walked closer. Brooks held his ground, still searching those silver eyes. Bending down, eyes up, he grabbed a sturdy piece of deadwood at his feet.

"You don't have to fight me Brandon. We're friends, remember."

Brandon walked closer, blade hanging in his left hand.

Brooks called out again, "You don't have to fight *me*. Fight it." He began to speak more urgently sensing that his time was short. "It tried to get me too . . . hold on to yourself. You don't have to let it control you."

Carlee, crouched close to the ground and slipped a little farther back into the woods, still unnoticed by Brandon. She watched, paralyzed, as the scene unfolded before her. Brandon stepped into the fighting ring.

Brooks began to hear the soft whispering voices. *Take us in. Take us into you. We want to be a part of you. You want us.*

Brooks shuddered, *I must still be somewhat infected*, he thought quickly.

Brooks stood, one hand holding the deadwood and the other fingering the zipper of his pants pocket. The two former friends now faced each other about three feet apart.

"You are one of us Brandon, not one of them. I know. I remember the real Brandon. I know how it feels. You can escape too. You have to choose to fight it."


The fish were beginning to bang the surface of the ice again. His mind was swimming with them. Bump. Bump. They knocked their heads against the Silver ice that carpeted the pond. More fish gathered, creating an urgency. Bump. Bump.

His memories sought, fought to become alive.

The ice held.


Brandon lifted up his blade and swung down towards Brook's head. Brooks stepped aside and the blade cut cleanly through the air, touching nothing. Brooks stepped back in front of him.

"You can't let them control you any longer, Brandon. You have to fight them. Don't fight me. Fight the Silver. IT IS YOUR LIFE!"

More fish rose to the surface banging against the ice.


Brandon raised his blade again. Stepping towards Brooks, he swung a horizontal arc. Brooks threw himself back and the blade sizzled as it cut through air, inches in front of his face. Brandon attacked again. Swinging and slicing. Brooks continued to step back, ducking and swerving. Then, Brooks felt the firmness of a tree against his back. Brandon paused; sensing his prey at a disadvantage, with two hands he brought the Silver sword singing towards him. Brooks dove to the side at the same time bringing the piece of wood smashing into Brandon's legs. He hit the ground with a thud and rolled quickly to a standing position. Brandon buckled. Brooks brought the wood back up and swung it, down striking Brandon across the back. The wood connected with flesh, splaying Brandon across the forest floor, splattering Silver everywhere.

As he fell, a small garbled cry escaped Brandon's lips. Pain.

Pain forced Brandon to become aware . . . of himself. His back screamed in agony. The ice began to crack. The Silver recoiled inward and frantically began to repair the cracks in the fortress that held Brandon's mind captive.

Brooks swung again.

Crack!

Brandon's body tried to get up but flopped forward onto the ground. Immediately, huge welts started forming across the back of his head where the wood had made contact.

Carlee cried out, "Stop it, Brooks! You're hurting him!"

She ran out and grabbed his arm as he wound up for another swing—this one aimed to connect with Brandon's shoulders.

"Let go! Look! The pain is helping Brandon come alive. They are fighting for control. I can hear them."

Carlee looked uncertainly at Brooks and let go of his arm.

"Trust me."

Carlee looked into Brooks' eyes. For the first time she *really* looked. She saw a young man growing there, and something stirred. She stepped back.

"Ok, I trust you."

Brooks turned his attention back to Brandon. He lifted up his stick again, but didn't see the flash of Silver until it was too late.

# Chapter Thirty Three

1:48 pm

The officers drove through Lower Fairview slowly.

"We'll never find them you know."

The skinny officer nodded. "Maybe."

"Then why are we driving down here?" He looked out the window as a homeless individual staggered by. "This area is such a dump. The city should just doze the whole place down and put the area out of its misery."

"Hmmm . . ."

They continued to drive in silence. Skinny turned the car east and then south towards the river.

"Where are we going?" the bald officer asked again. Constable Skinny looked over at Baldy.

"The river area. There are tons of places to hide and this is always where we find homeless people camping out. Besides," he stated slowly, "I have a hunch. I used to hang out down by the trestle bridge and climb underneath the beams and into the tunnels—it was a good hiding spot."

"So . . ."

"So, it may be where these kids are hiding, too." He met the incredulous look on Baldy's face. "You never know."

"That is stupid. There is water, sewage, and runoff in those tunnels. I'm not going in there. A kid wouldn't go in there. He'd get all wet and sick or something. Stupid." He shook his head. "Stupid. I'm not going in there."

Skinny pulled the car over to the curb along the road overlooking the river. The old trestle bridge was to their right. The sun was out and the day was mild. The trestles' oil-stained wood was like painted black strokes against the clear sky.

Both cops opened their doors and got out. Skinny pulled up his pants while Baldy adjusted his cap. They both walked along the bike trail to stand on the trestle. Leaning over the edge, they watched the river flowing beneath them.

"It's nice out." Skinny fingered his skinny moustache.

"Yup."

Skinny pointed to the sewer water barely crawling out of the tunnel opening. The rebar gate hung open on its hinge, resting against the cement wall.

"The gate is open, and there are clothes hanging from it," commented Skinny thoughtfully. Baldy rose up on his toes and rocked onto his heels.

"So . . . I'm still not going in there."

"You can't get in there from here, bonehead. Look at the slime covering the cement. How would you navigate it?" Skinny paused. "However, it looks like someone maybe *could've* been in there . . . I know another way in. Follow me."

Baldy looked uncertain and followed.

"I am not going in there," he said under his breath.


The cops followed the bike path past the trestle and into the trees. They followed it until they came to a spot where the trees opened and they could see the river again. The ground rose about five meters above the river. There was a bench for folks to rest, where they could watch the river flow by. Skinny crossed in front of Baldy and circumvented the bench. Picking his way along the ridge through the trees, he finally stopped at an old mound of cement raised up with a manhole cover at its short summit. The cover was rusted completely, and the area was a tangle of wild stinkweed and bramble. Skinny had already cleared the area and was heaving on the manhole cover when Baldy thrashed his way in. His forehead was beaded with sweat like a just-rinsed supermarket tomato. Frustrated and tired, he leaned forward on his knees, and through deep breaths tried to survey his partner's actions.

Shaking his head, he stepped up onto the mound, gripped the rusted grates of the manhole cover and said, "One, two, three."

They heaved until the heavy, rusted plate of iron gave way. As they dragged it across the cement, the flat, grinding sound ended with a bang as they dropped it to the ground.

"I'm not going in there."

Skinny ignored the comment. He dropped quickly into the hole and shimmied down the ladder. At the last rung, he hung and dropped into the dank smelling sewer. He looked up at Baldy, his eyes still not accustomed to the dark.

"Are you coming?"

Baldy shook his head in exasperation and dropped slowly into the sewer.

"I'm not staying down here long, you hear?"


After a beat, each of them stepped forward. The move from light to utter darkness was swift, and they had to pause to allow their eyes to adjust.

"Why is this manhole here? It seems like an odd place to have one." Baldy asked.

Skinny's eyes sparkled as memories of his youth flooded back. He answered, "I think the city guys had this one built for when the river floods. There are a few of them along the riverbanks here in the trees. They must have been added on after the sewer system was in place because they connect at sharp angles to the main tunnel system. We discovered this one one summer while exploring the riverbed for golf balls to sell. My buds and I used to dream up huge adventures down here. It wouldn't surprise me if Brandon's friends are also having an adventure down here."

They began to walk. Flashlights on, they quickly went through the flood tunnel and turned sharply into the main system. They were immediately assaulted with the pungent smell of stale slime and musty sludge.

Skinny stopped and glared down both ways of the tunnel, looking for clues of any kind. Stepping farther, Skinny lifted his flashlight and shone it on the walls.

"Look at this?" Baldy quickly joined him.

"The mud has been scraped away here," Skinny said slowly, "Fresh?"

"I think so. Look, there's more."

They both examined the sides of the tunnel and found scrapes on both sides. They scoured the floor, their police instincts kicking in hard.

"Over here." Skinny trudged over. "A heel print. It's pointed west." Baldy was pointing to the ground.

Skinny slapped Baldy hard on the back, "Way to go! Let's move."

Like hounds on the hunt, the two cops followed the scrape marks deeper into the tunnel system.

# Chapter Thirty Four

The red glow lit up Keenan's face as he peered over the rock. There were hundreds of them. All were just alike, but in various lengths and widths. Together, they resembled a tangle of snakes as they slithered and squirmed in their entwinement.

Smack!

Keenan was sucked back into the swirling madness. He was discovered. Whips of Red slashed around the whirlpool looking for Keenan, without any luck. For Keenan was no longer material nor matter. He was but a wisp. A thought. A soul. Diving and swirling, Keenan dove for another black hole in the whirlpool of Red.

Again, Keenan was thrown through a filmy boundary and into the past of the Red Toxinate. A maelstrom of emotion hit him with the strength of a hurricane. Anger flared and roared. At first, Keenan thought it was directed at him, but then, as he continued to be unaffected, he realized it was the memory itself that he was witnessing. Men in steel outfits, armed with steel nets and cages, were tearing into the nest of Red Toxinate. Left and right, men were being whipped and tossed about. Blood mixed with Toxinate created a blinding storm of red.

Keenan manoeuvred to better see the result of the slaughter. Then one man came staggering out of the sea carrying a locked cage. Wrapped around him were whips of Red lashing and strangling. This man, bound by Red, stumbled towards a steel machine. He held his hands outstretched as if begging for someone to help him. The Red continued to lacerate his body. A step before the large steel machine door, the man fell face first into the rock. The sound of his nose breaking caused Keenan to cringe. An arm reached through the door and grabbed the cage; the door closed. The man was left to die.

All Keenan saw was red.

He was sucked out again into the whirlpool. Red continued to search for him, raking blindly through itself. Keenan floated and thought absently. Floating in and out of memories was doing nothing to help him regain control. Yet when he first abandoned his body and dove into this abyss he knew there was a hope in this whirlpool somewhere.

Then it hit him.

He would have to control the Red from the inside, in order to gain control of himself. He would control the Red controlling him. It was an abstract way of thinking about it, but it was the only way he could think of to survive. He dove in deeper. All whirlpools empty into something, he thought. Black holes whipped by him. Each held an untold story. Keenan ignored them all and continued his descent into Red's soul.

*     *     *

The Silver lashed out like a ball of flame at Brooks' feet. The contact was hard and complete. Brooks' ankles fractured with the impact. He crumpled to the ground. Brandon loomed menacingly over Brooks, then crouched with fingers outstretched, grabbed Brooks by the neck and began to squeeze.

The Silver flowed from Brandon over to Brooks. Through the 'slime', Brooks grabbed Brandon's arms and tried to pry them away from his neck. Brandon was relentless.

Desperate, Brooks pulled his head back and butted it hard against Brandon's forehead. A web of pain flooded his vision, but he was rewarded when the grip on his neck lessened. He used the moment of respite to pull more air into his burning lungs, then rolled out from underneath Brandon. But Brandon wouldn't release him.

Brandon's eyes closed and then opened. Vacant. Again. He stood, bringing a dangling Brooks with him. His feet hung limply from his legs. Brandon began to press his thumbs firmly into Brooks' throat. Brooks squirmed, but with no ground to give him purchase, he was like a worm, dangling on a hook.

Silver continued to pour over him. Gasping and sputtering, Brooks was slowly being overcome. It flowed into his open mouth and eyes. The familiar sensation was not comforting. The battle for his mind began again, but this time the battle for breath was much more important. Black began to mist like a dark fog at the edges of his mind. He was fading. The fog moved in closer. His vision began to disappear; the last thing he saw was Brandon's vacant eyes twinkling with Silver as they crushed the life out of him.

Carlee huddled in the bushes watching Brandon as he began to crush Brooks. She felt hopeless. Tears streamed unbidden down her face. Her matted hair hung over her eyes as she helplessly watched Brooks' limp body fall to the ground. Something inside her boiled over. This could not happen.

Her scream pierced the forest. She ran up to Brandon and hit him repeatedly with the garbage can lid while jumping on his back, trying to pull him off. Silver immediately began to crawl over her.

Although the sensation was new to her, the ferocity of her emotions quickly overpowered the Silver's intent. She screamed again in anger as she pounded her fists on Brandon's back.

"Get off of him! Get off him! You'll kill him! Stop it. Stop it. Stop it!"

Tears fell from her chin, landing on Brandon.

Immediately, the Silver in that spot vanished into steam.

Carlee didn't notice. She continued to beat Brandon on his head and back, tears and spit falling like rain on his body. The air began to fill with steam. She could feel Brandon's grip on Brooks loosening. The Silver was quickly fleeing her body, leaving her untouched.

Brooks dropped to the ground. He curled into the fetal position. His body shook as he raggedly sucked in breath after precious breath.

Each tear, infused with her emotion, burned his skin. Each tear had stung his brain. Each sting brought a memory closer to breaking the surface. Brandon began to stand. Steam rose from his back while his eyes searched and rolled in their sockets. His hands lay limp at his side. The fight for control ensued.

Carlee cradled Brooks in her arms, sobbing and sobbing, oblivious to the effects of her tears. Kneeling closer, she listened for breathing.

Nothing.

Silver swarmed all over his face and body as though he had landed in a phosphorescent anthill. Carlee knelt closer. Instinctively she brought her lips to his mouth and kissed him. Her tears rolled down her cheeks and coursed their way into her kiss. The tears travelled into Brooks' mouth, past his lips and across his tongue. Each tear renting a path for life. The tears slipped down his throat. Steam began to come out of his mouth and Carlee withdrew quickly, unsure of what had just happened. She knelt, holding Brooks' hand, and continued to cry. More steam rose from his mouth as the tears coated his esophagus and lungs. He began to cough.

His body convulsed slightly, and Carlee gasped. His body curled up violently. He turned his head to the side and vomited. Silver splattered the ground.

Carlee let a smile break through her tears. She grabbed his face in her hands and looked him in the eyes. His eyes were clear. Seeing Brooks there, really there, Carlee smiled more broadly. Her wet cheeks were hot against Brooks as she pulled him closer to herself. Wiping off his face, hands in his hair, she kissed him on the forehead. Brooks smiled. Carlee smiled slightly and turned her head a little in embarrassment.

Then it hit. Brooks buckled over as the pain from his broken ankles rushed to the forefront of his senses.

A voice carried over to both of them.

"Brooks?" Brandon's mouth twisted as he forced out the word.

\*    \*    \*

Skinny and Baldy came to the rope hanging down from the manhole. They had passed the pile of clothes and other stuff taken from Kendra's home. They saw the shattered cement wall and were cautiously moving forward. Guns were out and ready. It was here at the rope that they finally called in. Silver Toxinate was splattered everywhere. A sliced through garbage can lid lay on the ground, and signs of struggle were evident.

"Corporal James and the Chief are on their way. They called in back up . . . the works. Even the army was called in."

"You're sure this is the stuff, eh?" Baldy asked cautiously.

"Absolutely, it has to be."

Baldy boosted Skinny and the two of them hefted their uniformed bodies up the ladder, into the sunlight.

# Chapter Thirty Five

The descent continued. Deeper and deeper he dove. At last he found the centre. The turbulence was now behind him. Here it was calm. Here it was thick. Here was its soul.

At first Keenan thought it was just a void. Then, as he adjusted to what was around him, he saw that it was more. Scenes of Red's rocky home and then scenes of violence flashed like movie screens around him. Each scene a reflection of what the Red was feeling. Keenan floated into the middle. The scenes encircled him, flashing, changing constantly. In the middle was an orb. It glowed, emitting a soft blue light. It waited.

Outside, Dolan began to get worried. He had watched Keenan throw himself to the ground and against the walls, tearing his shirt to shreds. Now he lay still. Dead still. Red continued to whip in and around his body. Dolan stayed crouched and watched. Afraid for himself. Afraid for his brother. Afraid.

Keenan came closer. Closer. He could feel the glow. It had warmed. This was it. This was the only way to gain back the control he had lost. To gain back himself. Although . . . Keenan didn't want to face the possible consequences . . . His soul stared directly into his enemy's soul. Both matterless and yet both in their most real and true state. This was the moment. He floated closer. He reached out. The orb glowed brighter as he delicately reached in and pulled out. He felt seared and burnt. It was foreign. Wrong. Not human.

Dolan watched Keenan's back rise off the ground and slam down again. He didn't know what was happening, but something wasn't right. Keenan's midsection lifted again and smacked again onto the ground. Dolan rose to a standing position.

This was it. If he dove in, there was no turning back. He knew this instinctively. Could he win? The question loomed in front of him. What choice did he have? He had to. He had to in order to save Dolan. He had to in order to save others. He had to in order to save himself. He had to. *God, help me*, he thought. Keenan plunged himself, his soul, into the blue orb.

Heat seared, scorched and stripped him of everything he was.

He was there.

Somewhere.

Naked. As naked as a soul could be. His soul bared.

In that nakedness, Keenan saw himself reflected. In front of him stretched a sea of water. Behind him, a path of clay stones leading into darkness. He stepped to the edge. Water lapped at his feet.

Then he appeared. Rising out of the water to stand calmly . . . it was himself. He saw himself, or a reflection of himself standing there among the unsettled waters. His unruly dark hair danced around his ears and his black eyes stared right back at him. Thinking it a mirror, he lifted his arm. The reflection of him did not. He looked around. He was alone.

Keenan studied the image more closely. He observed greasy stains streaking across his face and shoulders. He saw pockets of pus growing, bursting, leaking, and starting all over again.

Keenan was confused. He just stood there. This wasn't what he expected. Was this Red emulating himself, or was this . . . him? He just stood. And so did the image of him—still and unflinching. Keenan looked down at his hand. In between his forefinger and thumb he held a match. Keenan looked up again. Himself was still staring back at him. Leaning down he struck the match on the clay stones. A pure flame lit and burned brightly, casting no shadows. He watched the flame burn, but it did not burn out. Keenan stepped forward. His reflection stood. He stepped out into the water and found that he could walk over it, the waves still lapping at his feet. A few more steps brought Keenan face to face with his image. Keenan held out the match. His reflection looked back at him. Disconcerted, he tossed the match into the water. He looked up and there it was again between his forefinger and his thumb. Acting purely on instinct, he stepped forward to the image of himself and placed the match up to the figure in front of him. The flame licked the hair, but did not catch. He brought the match up close to a greasy stain across the shoulders.

The grease caught fire.

Keenan immediately dropped the match and began to grab at his chest and shoulder trying to put out the flame. His reflection stood still. Burning. The fire was hot and furious. Not in a way of singeing flesh, but an internal fire—far stronger, far purer.

Then it was done.

Keenan looked at himself standing in front of him, staring back at him. He saw the stain removed, and in its place pure, soft skin. Keenan looked down and there, again, the match was burning in his fingers. *That hurt*, he thought. *But, it also feels . . . free.*

Light.

He quickly placed the match up to another stain across his chest and stomach.

Again the intense heat and internal fire. He cried out involuntarily at the pain, gasping, doubling over, and then it was done. In its place was smooth skin. Keenan shook his head and a smile twitched at his lip. He felt clean. He lifted the match to the pus-filled sores. The sores caught fire and smouldered inward like the end of a cigar.

Again the internal fire burned. Burned and burned and burned. The fire travelled from one sore to the next. Keenan fell to his knees on the water and stopped resisting the pain. He bowed his head and gave himself over to the fire. Immediately, his body erupted in flames. Stains burned, sores popped and boiled. Time ceased to exist and the changes in him were measured through waves of intensity. The heat was fierce, the purging complete.

After what seemed like a thousand years, though maybe only seconds, Keenan lifted his eyes. The sea before him was shining pure gold and there was no longer a reflection of him anywhere. He looked down at his arms and hands and legs.

They shone like polished bronze. New. Free.

Tears coursed down his cheeks and he stood. He walked out onto the golden sea. A sword, polished and sharpened, hovered over the water. On the hilt was engraved his name. He began to cry. Not

Keenan, but his real name—the name that was him in his entirety. He placed his hand on the hilt and it all disappeared.

Keenan stood in a ring of fire. Walls of fire rose up around him. He was clothed again. His feet were standing in sand. Hot, dry sand. Beyond the fire was blackness. The light of the fire reflected in the blade of his sword. A flash of blinding Red whisked into the circle. Sand blew up into the air, swirling and being sucked into the fire.

Keenan instinctively covered his face and took his stance. His legs spread apart, and he flicked his head to get the hair out of his eyes. The sand settled. A serpent, deep blood red rose out from the sandy mist. Its eyes were black and full of hate. Its tongue snapped in and out searching for its prey. The scales along the serpent's back were horned and pointed, giving off a red glow. Black oozed and dripped from the corner of the serpent's mouth and slipped like raindrops staining the sand.

Keenan stood firm. The serpent raised itself up higher, twisting and undulating back and forth like a pendulum.

Keenan stood. His eyes following the serpent's every move.

The serpent studied him and then he heard his own voice come out of the serpent's mouth.

"I own you." Keenan shook his head.

"I own you. You gave yourself to me. We could rule this body together. You and I."

Its tongue whipped and hissed with every word.

"Remember the feeling of that power—it is yours to control."

Black ooze dropped to the ground.

*"I own you," the serpent hissed.*

Keenan's eyes followed it as it soaked into the black circle. A painful choice. The serpent struck. Keenan felt its fangs sink into his leg severing his muscle and tendon. He turned and slashed with his sword, the serpent dodged easily and continued to swing back and forth.

"I own you and I will kill you. You will become my flesh."

Keenan felt the sticky blackness of the ooze spreading up his leg. Laying the sword on his wound, he began to slide the sharp edge of the sword along the wound.

"Killing yourself for me are you?" the serpent hissed. The black ooze melted from his leg and left the wound open and bleeding.

Keenan's eyes lit on fire.

"You will not do that again."

He grabbed his sword with both hands and faced off with the serpent. The serpent hissed angrily and dove again for his body.

Keenan didn't move, but simply struck out with the sword. Red dived to the side, and Keenan slashed again. He missed on his downward slash, but on the way up caught the underside of the monster with the tip of his sword. The serpent's skin peeled back and black ooze spurted out. The serpent roared with anger. It drove its head to the left and to the right, lashing and striking. Keenan swung hard and fast, his feet moving as the serpent danced and weaved. Strike after strike, slash after slash.

Keenan's shoulders were bleeding now and the hilt of his sword was slick with blood. Black ooze covered the sandy ground from the many slashes in the serpent's underside. And still the serpent fought. Taunting, the serpent laughed and continued to offer him power and control.

"You don't have to fight! Stop and we'll share the power. We can control together. We'll become one. We'll work as one."

The words had little effect when he focused on the fight at hand. When he focused on the black ooze, the words affected him. He would begin to slip, fall, and make clumsy attempts at battle. These moments cost him flesh. These moments cost him blood.

After another slip on the ooze, Keenan was down on his knees. He brought his sword up in defence. Sand was sticking to his sweating body and irritating the wounds. Keenan struggled to his feet. His breath was ragged and he gasped. This had to end. He stood, blinked the sweat out of his eyes and focused. The taunting words of the serpent began to fade out and his vision centred on the serpents eyes. *That is where I will strike.* He stood shakily and lifted up the sword. Blood ran down his arms and onto his chest.

He looked into the serpents black, pinned eyes and spoke in a calm voice, "You will die."

The serpent roared, reared his head back and drove down, its bared fangs glinting and dripping with Keenan's blood.

Keenan pointed his sword in the serpent's direction.

Dolan stepped closer to Keenan's body lying on the tunnel floor. Slashes and open wounds began to appear across his chest and thighs. Blood soaked into the sludge staining the ground. Dolan knelt by his side. Keenan's eyes were closed, but Dolan could see his eyes flipping back and forth in their sockets. Something was going on inside. Dolan grabbed Keenan's hand and held it. A tear formed in his eye and dropped onto their hands.

Sitting cross-legged, holding his hand, Dolan whispered, "I'm here, Keenan, buddy. I'm sorry. I'm so sorry. Come back to me, Keenan. Come back."

He bowed his head and wept.

# Chapter Thirty Six

Suddenly the serpent began to sizzle. Vapours rose from its back. Drops of rain began to fall on its head. Around him, the walls of fire began to sputter, and water began to soak through the sand. Distracted, the serpent pulled back leaving its left eye exposed.

Keenan struck.

He sprung into the air and drove his sword straight into the eye of the serpent, burying it to the hilt. He let go and dropped to the ground. The serpent roiled and curled. Screeched and screamed. Twisted and smacked its head on the ground trying to dislodge the sword. Black ooze sprayed out of the punctured eye like a fountain. The body of the serpent began to cave in on itself,—shrinking and collapsing. Water started to rise, seeping up through the sand and extinguishing the surrounding fire. His sword fell out of the serpent's socket. It dropped to the ground and stuck into the sand, the hilt wobbling from the impact. The serpent twisted towards Keenan. Its good eye piercing, hate-filled and burning. It opened its mouth to speak. The rain was causing a mist, clear and fresh. The serpent was disintegrating.

Then . . . it died. It's head fell to the ground at the feet of Keenan. It's body shriveled and deflated.

The waters rose, covering the sand and leaving no trace of the Red.

Keenan lifted his face upwards, the rain washing him, pouring over him, wiping away all traces of the fight. Keenan lifted up his hands and fell to his knees.

And then Keenan was flushed out of the blackness and slammed back into his own body.

The last thing he saw was his sword, point down, slowly being enveloped by the rising water.

Keenan's eyes popped open. He could feel his heart beating. He felt burning wounds all over his body. Keenan breathed. Stale air passed over his tongue, into his lungs and out again. Deeper. His chest rose. A smile crept onto his face. He was alive. He was himself. Turning, he saw Dolan holding his hand and staring at him.

"Hey," Keenan said softly.

"Hey."

Abruptly, Keenan turned onto his side and grasped his throat. He pulled on the Red whip around his throat and body. The Red, wilted like a piece of yarn, unravelled itself from him. He dropped it to the ground.

A ball of tangled Red Toxinate lay on the floor. There was no glow left. It was motionless, lifeless.

Keenan laid down again, resting his arms beside him. "That feels better."

Dolan laughed. They looked at each other, their eyes confirming a brotherhood that never truly existed before.

"I thought you were gone, you know."

Keenan let out a breath of air, "Yeah, me too, bro. Me too."

They turned their heads at the sound of feet pounding through the tunnels.

"We're over here!" Dolan shouted, "Hey!"

Around the corner came men dressed in army gear, white cages strapped to their backs, each carrying a black shield in front of their full headgear.

Dolan stood, grimacing a bit and lifted up his hands. "It's finished, we're all done here. It's dead. My brother killed it."

He gestured to Keenan lying slashed and beaten, yet smiling on the ground. They were quickly surrounded by the men with shields; Corporal James elbowed his way into the circle. With a quick look, he ignored the boys and studied the lump of tangled Red.

"This is it," he said more to himself than to anyone else. He fingered the hair coming out of his nose and knelt down closer to inspect the Red puddle.

"Did you finally capture the Toxinate Corporal?" Chief Ruther's voice carried easily in the tunnels.

He was standing outside the circle, up on his tippy toes, trying to see over the black shields. The men awaited a command from their Corporal.

"Well done, men. Well done. Roadhouse, package up this Red Toxinate and have it sent immediately to the lab. The rest of you continue scouring the tunnels for the Silver." A surly man stepped forward and began to cautiously remove the Red.

The Corporal glanced down at Keenan lying on the ground.

"Get out of the way son, this is Federal business and you are obstructing an investigation."

"Chief Ruther." The Chief acknowledged the command. "I've captured the Red Toxinate. Make sure these boys are taken in for questioning. Press charges if need be. I want no more trouble."

The Chief nodded.

With no more than a "Humph," and a scratch of his hairy chest, he led the troops farther into the tunnels.

# Chapter Thirty Seven

2:21 pm

$B$ang!

A bullet whistled through the air and thumped Brandon squarely in the chest knocking him flat to the ground. Brooks and Carlee instinctively ducked. Another bullet whistled through the air, thunking loudly into a tree. Carlee screamed and rushed to Brandon throwing, herself in front of him.

Shouts of anger arose from the police as they rushed into the scene. Skinny and Baldy were there, Chief Ruther coming out of the manhole, and six other officers. All guns were trained on Carlee.

A mega-phoned voice broke over the din, "Get out of the way. You are obstructing justice. I repeat, GET OUT OF THE WAY!"

Carlee lowered herself down and knelt beside Brandon.

"Carlee, get out of the way—they'll shoot!"

Brook's voice was desperate.

He turned to the cops, sitting up and waving his hands, tears streaming down his face. He starting shouting, "Don't shoot, Don't shoot her. Please don't shoot her!"

Carlee looked into Brandon's face. In his eyes, there was a tiny spark.

"Carlee . . ." The voice was hoarse and gargled.

"Shhhh . . . don't speak," Carlee whispered, "You'll be ok. Just hold on, ok?"

Brandon shook his head, and Carlee looked down at the bullet wound. Blood, red and sparkling with Silver, bubbled from his wound. She looked back at Brandon. Blood and Silver began to leak out of his mouth.

"Carlee," he began. Then choking on his own blood, he sputtered some more, "I'm so sorry. Tell them Carlee. Please."

Carlee, nodded. Tears streamed down her own face. The cops were surrounding her now, watching. Brandon choked once more, and his eyes rolled back into his head. His chest convulsed, and he was gone.

"Noooooo!"

A cop grabbed Carlee from behind as she went to throw herself on Brandon.

Brooks sat there, feeling useless. He cried, his shoulders shaking.

The Silver glowed and crawled over its victim, savouring the last remnants of life as the cops swarmed in to quarantine the area.

# Chapter Thirty Eight

1 week later

"So that's it, eh?" Tyler shook his head and crossed his feet up on the kitchen table, adjusting the cigarette in his mouth. He looked at Keenan carefully. There was something different about his brother now . . . he was . . . more sure of himself. He even carried himself differently . . . *Something else happened that he isn't telling me,* Tyler thought to himself.

Brooks was in a wheelchair with both legs in casts, Carlee beside him holding his hand with both of hers.

"Yeah," Keenan answered quietly, "That's it."

Dolan, stood and grabbed a glass from the sink, wiped it out with his shirt, and filled it with water. His ribs were bound tightly and he had his shirt off.

"Keenan saved my life," he looked at Keenan and nodded.

"I barely saved my own life, let alone yours," Keenan answered back. He kept his fight with the Red serpent to himself. If it wasn't for the gauze bandages covering up all his wounds, he would've thought the entire episode was a dream.

Carlee spoke up, "Brandon's mom . . . how is she?" Lori wrapped her arms around Keenan, who was sitting cross-legged on the kitchen chair. "She's . . . struggling. She would want to hear your story again, I think. There are still some missing pieces for her."

"You know what kills me?" Dolan asked, setting the water down.

The group waited.

"Brandon may have won. He may have pulled out of it. I was the one that took him down there. I led him to the Silver and I couldn't lead him away. He was intoxinated because of me. Carlee—you said he was telling us sorry when he was dying . . ." Carlee nodded. "He could've won. There was still hope. If only those stupid cops . . ." He let the words hang. "There's always hope."

No one said anything in response.

"So there's none of this Silver stuff left at all?" Tyler pried softly, breaking the uncomfortable silence.

"NO!" Keenan and Carlee said at the same time.

Turning, they looked at each other and laughed.

# Epilogue

Crawling along the stump, the black beetle with a gold back searched for food. The ground was scorched, a black stain in the forest's memory. The fire had been deliberate and thorough. Nothing survived in the quarantined area. The beetle's antennae quivered back and forth as its senses searched for food. Despite the barrenness, it ventured across a stretch of black ash and into a small patch of scorched grass on the other side. The antennae straightened and the beetle followed its instincts. Skittering quickly forward, it circumvented a few blades and stopped. Just ahead was a small, glowing drop.

Of Silver.